XOUTH, THE APE

Xouth, The Ape
A Tale of Manners

Iakovos Pitsipios

Translated by
Neo G. Christodoulides

OpenBook Publishers

https://www.openbookpublishers.com

©2025 Neo G. Christodoulides (Translation, Introductions and Notes)

Open Book Classics vol. 13 | ISSN: 2054-216X (Print); 2054-2178 (Online)

ISBN Paperback: 978-1-80511-717-9
ISBN Hardback: 978-1-80511-718-6
ISBN PDF: 978-1-80511-719-3
ISBN HTML: 978-1-80511-721-6
ISBN EPUB: 978-1-80511-720-9
DOI: https://doi.org/10.11647/OBP.0493

Cover image: Anonymous, 'A Giant Monkey in Uniform Holding up Pierrot and a Man with a Whip' (after 1825), Lithograph touched with pen and brown ink and graphite. Metropolitan Museum of Art, New York, https://commons.wikimedia.org/wiki/File:A_Giant_Monkey_in_Uniform_Holding_up_Pierrot_and_a_Man_with_a_Whip_MET_DP808176.jpg
Cover design: Jeevanjot Kaur Nagpal

Contents

Foreword

Neo G. Christodoulides

Xouth, The Ape: A Tale of Manners is set in the first half of the nineteenth century, when the newly founded Hellenic Kingdom (1832) tried to find its place on the world map. It relates the fictionalised adventures of the German travel writer Jakob Salomon Bartholdy, who, in this narrative, was transformed into an ape for his sins and subsequently passed between various Greek masters to serve as a butler.

The novel is a biting satire of the post-revolutionary Greek elites, a visceral attack on a society that tentatively tried to forge its identity between 'East' and 'West,' modernity and antiquity. It also engages with Western attitudes towards and perceptions of Greece, as manifested through the works of German, English and French contemporary intellectuals—or pseudointellectuals—who established the custom of travelling extensively to Greece to 'discover' and to 'describe' the 'real' Hellenic culture, and the 'true' character and customs of its people, in a patronising, downright colonialising manner.

Towards the end of the novel, Anaxagoras Ligarides—a conceited aspiring Greek travel writer—boasts of having written a travelogue on Egypt in the 'European fashion,' in which he preposterously claims to have been the first to climb the pyramids in 1835. But his wise uncle swiftly grounds him by reminding him that tens of thousands had climbed the pyramids for centuries!

The wise man's commonsensical remark evocatively foreshadows the words of the Nigerian novelist Chinua Achebe (1930–2023), a fiercely outspoken voice against the colonial and Eurocentric representation of Africa: 'Westerners always claim to have discovered Nigeria in the sixteenth century, but Nigeria was always there!'

In the eyes of the novel's author Iakovos Pitsipios, Kallistratos Evgenides, the owner of Xouth, is the archetypal nouveau-riche Athenian who spins his narrative of an imagined pedigree that includes resistance fighters and reaches back to antiquity, while incessantly mimicking (aping) the latest European trends and fashions. Evgenides' naivety in political matters—he is a supporter of the 'Megali Idea,' an irredentist national movement that was to prove disastrous for the Hellenic state in the twentieth century—as well as his shallowness and self-referentiality represent his entire generation and social class.

Not much is known about the novel's author, Iakovos Pitsipios. His date of birth is not certain (1800? 1802? 1803?), nor is the pronunciation of his surname (Πιτσιπιός? Πιτσίπιος? Πιτζίπιος?). We know that he was born in Chios and moved to Constantinople (Istanbul) after the Ottomans destroyed the island in 1822 during the Greek Revolution.

We also know that he was—at least for a time—Catholic, and an ardent supporter of the Catholic Church (Fairey, 2013). He taught French in Hermoupolis, the capital of Syros, as a teacher at the Greek Orthodox School, where he also published the literary magazine *Αποθήκη των Τερπνών και Ωφελίμων Γνώσεων* ('The Storehouse of Delightful and Useful Knowledge').

His support for the Roman Catholic Church brought him into conflict with the Greek Orthodox Church, and he eventually left his post under obscure circumstances. He subsequently worked for the Ottoman Imperial administration in Constantinople. In Rome, he wrote a pamphlet on behalf of the Roman Catholic Church, published in 1852 as *L' Église Orientale*.

Pitsipios' death in 1869 is also shrouded in mystery. His body was found in the Bosporus, and the circumstances of his death remain unclear. A newspaper at the time, *Εκλεκτική* of 30 September 1869, speculated that 'he might have either been killed by the Turks or the popish' ('ΥποτΙθεται Οτι εδολοφονΗθη ή εκ ΤοΥρκων ή εκ ΠαπιστΩν').

The lengthy article even mentioned the twenty-page manuscript of a satirical poem titled 'Αναργυριας ή ΑπΟκρυφα ΚωνσταντινουπΟλεως,' which the demised carried in his pocket, implying that Iakovos Pitsipios was a well-known figure in his time.

In 1839, Pitsipios published Ἡ Ὀρφανὴ τῆς Χίου ἢ Ὁ Θρίαμβος τῆς ἀρετῆς ('The Orphan of Chios or the Triumph of Virtue') in Ermoupolis, the capital of Syros.

Xouth, The Ape first appeared in serialised form in 1848 but seems to have soon fallen into oblivion. The general lack of interest in this work is even more surprising as it dealt with a topic so hotly debated in Greek intellectual circles of the time: namely, Western travellers' perception and portrayal of the Hellenic world. The novel did not enter the Greek literary canon perhaps because its author was Catholic in a country whose establishment identified as Greek Orthodox.

Interest in the author and his work has revived in recent years. Two editions of Pitsipios' novels were published in Greece in the nineties by Nasos Vagenas and Dimitris Tziovas, respectively: *Ἰάκωβος Γ. Πιτσιπίος 'Ο Πίθηκος Ξουθ ἤ Τα ἤθη του αιώνος' Φιλολογική επιμέλεια Νάσος Βαγενάς, Εκδόσεις Νεφέλη, Αθήνα* (1995) and *Ἰάκωβος Γ. Πιτζίπιος 'Ἡ Ορφανή της Χίου και ο Πίθηκος Ξουθ' Φιλολογική επιμέλεια, Δημήτρης Τζιόβας, Εκδόσεις Ουράνη, Αθήνα* (1995).

In addition, Pitsipios received the attention of Hellenic scholarship outside Greece (Roilos, O'Neil). *Xouth, the Ape* recently found its way into the educational canon of Greek schools, and a play based on the book was even staged in 2022.

In translating this work from Greek into English, I strove to maintain the novel's polyglossic texture by alternating between an elevated, archaic style and a more colloquial variant used by the different characters. I believe that the heightened scholarly interest in this complex and enigmatic novel called for an English translation to make it accessible to a general readership.

A PDF of the original Greek text is available on the digital resources page for this book.[1]

Berchtesgaden, 2024

---

1   https://doi.org/10.11647/OBP.0493#resources

Introduction
The Literary Precursors of
Xouth, the Ape

By the nineteenth century, the novel was hardly a 'novel' genre anymore. It could trace its success story back to the late Renaissance, while its remarkable popularity in Europe did not display any signs of waning. Nonetheless, leading intellectuals of the time hesitated to embrace this genre, with the influential German philosopher, literary critic and playwright Friedrich Schiller (1759–1805) calling the novelist the 'half-brother of the poet' ('der Halbbruder des Dichters') (Schiller, p. 741).

The novel was hardly considered equal to poetry, drama or epic, mainly because Aristotle did not mention it in his *Poetics*. (Rebig, 1972, p. 12). And, of course, this would have been impossible since the earliest longer narrative prose works that we identify as 'novels' only appeared in the second century AD, long after Aristotle.

However, as the Russian philosopher and literary critic Mikhail Bakhtin (1895–1975) aptly observed, the novel could not have featured anywhere in the system laid out by Aristotle because the concept of the 'novel' defied and challenged the definitions 'of genre and statism' (Bakhtin, 1981, p. 8).

This literary genre benefited from the literary tradition that preceded it and widely deployed existing leitmotivs such as the 'recognition' ('anagnorisis') and analepsis already found in Homeric epic and the Greek tragedy. Nonetheless, despite the novel's remarkably protean qualities and its tenacious malleability, certain themes and leitmotivs stood the test of time. They have recurred from antiquity to the present age. These include the anagnorisis, the unreliable internal narrator and the travel narrative as subject matter.

 https://doi.org/10.11647/OBP.0493.00

Our earliest extant novel is Apuleius' *Metamorphoses* or *The Golden Ass* (*assinus aureus*). It is based on a now-lost Greek precursor called *Lucius or the Ass* (Λούκιος ἢ ὄνος) by the otherwise unknown Greek author Lucius of Patrae. The novel's protagonist and primary narrator, Lucius, is a curious drifter who roams the Eastern Mediterranean in his quest for adventure and easy gratification. Lucius meets witches and is transformed into an ass for his curiosity. He only regains his human shape towards the end of the novel, having been sold to various masters and having witnessed many scenes of natural and supernatural life. Lucius was to become the prototype for numerous Western novels from the Renaissance onwards that mainly appeared in Spain.

These novels came to be known as 'picaresque novels' (from *picaro*, meaning 'rogue'), and a notable example of this is the anonymous *Lazarillo de Tormes* (1554). The picaresque genre, a subcategory of the adventure novel, also flourished in different variations in the English-speaking world with authors like Henry Fielding (*Tom Jones*), Daniel Defoe (*Moll Flanders*), Laurence Sterne (*A Sentimental Journey*) and Mark Twain (*Adventures of Huckleberry Finn*). The hero of the picaresque novel usually travels extensively, endures many trials and tribulations, suffers setbacks and faces danger.

Travelling in space inevitably entails a time lapse. However, as Bakhtin so perceptively noted, ancient picaresque novels were not at all concerned with the hero›s development. Their novelistic time is static; there are no signs of ageing or decay, and the protagonists do not seem to change. (Bakhtin, 1986, pp. 10, 13, 15). Works like Apuleius' *The Golden Ass*, Heliodorus' *Aethiopica* and Tatius' *Leucippe and Clitophon* are all characterised by a lack of 'localisation and historicity' (Bakhtin, 1986, p. 15).

Interestingly, when we move to the eighteenth century and come to Voltaire's adventure novel *Candide* (1759), we surprisingly notice that when the eponymous hero finally finds his sweetheart Cunégonde, after many trials and tribulations, she is already old, and he finds her repulsive (Bakhtin, 1981, p. 90). This detail ushered in a new era of novelistic writing, a new kind of novel: the Bildungsroman. It is a real-time matrix where characters can grow physically and spiritually. Bakhtin calls this the novel of 'human emergence and development' (Bakhtin, 1981, pp. 11, 22, 23; Borghart & Temmerman, 2010, p. 47). In the Bildungsroman, the characters progress; they change and develop in real time and real space. Examples of the latter are Henry Fielding's *Tom Jones* (1749), Johann W. von Goethe's *Wilhelm Meisters Lehrjahre* (1795–1796) and Charles Dickens' *David Copperfield* (1849).

In Germany, this shift towards reality connected with the country's nationalist movement, and it is no wonder that Goethe himself—a friend of the philosopher of the German Enlightenment and the 'Sturm und Drang' movement that emphasised German nationalism, Johann Gottfried Herder—wrote a Bildungsroman. Again, Bakhtin notes that both Herder and Goethe lead us to a kind of novel where 'man is growing in national historical time' (Bakhtin, 1986, pp. 25, 49).

The Ape and the Mirror

The elusive, peculiar and widely imaginative novel *Xouth, The Ape: A Tale of Manners* (*Ο Πίθηκος Χούθ ή Τα ήθη του αιώνος*) is the only one of two known picaresque novels written in Greek in the nineteenth century—the other is Pavlos Kalligas' *Thanos Vlekas* of 1855—and the only one that uses the topos of therianthropy.

In its idiosyncratic structure, acidity, Rabelaisian humour and deft weaving of real and fictional events and persons, *Xouth, The Ape* remains unparalleled in the modern Greek literary canon. The fact that a part of it is lost—or was never finished—is one of the most regrettable facts of modern Greek literary history.

The novel has all the features of a Bildungsroman. The hero's actions are embedded in a real chronotope, a national historical time, with real places, events and persons. The scenes unfold in Smyrna and its fashionable suburb Vournova, Athens and the island of Syros, 'the most civilised place in Greece,' but also boldly move beyond the boundaries of the Hellenic world. Hence, our protagonists are seen in Egypt, New Orleans, New York, London and Paris in the prison of Sainte Pélagie.

Fittingly enough, for a novel that owes much to the literary genre of Milesian Tales (*milesiaca*), Smyrna plays a key role in the tale. Our hero first set foot in that city as the travel writer Jakob Bartholdy and was brought to the city for a second time as an ape.

Time in the novel is also real. When our protagonist encounters again his 'nemesis,' the cunning 'Countess Avendrote,' thirty years after she had deceived him and set his calamities in motion, he notes with satisfaction that she has become an old hag. In addition, notable events of modern Greek history, like the 'European Loan' (Treaty of London, 1832), feature abundantly in the background of the narration. The text is fastidiously filled with time references: we are told that the travelogue that would prove a *cause célèbre* and the downfall of our hero was published in 1805, and that thirty years pass between our protagonist's two visits to Smyrna—the first as a man, the second as an ape. The fictional meeting between Jakob Bartholdy and Adamantios Koraes was set in 1823.

The protagonists of the novel are based on real historical figures. Jakob Bartholdy is based on Jakob Salomon Bartholdy (1779–1825), a Prussian diplomat born in the Jewish faith but converted to Protestantism. The historical Bartholdy travelled extensively through Greece while still under Ottoman rule and wrote a critical travelogue of the Hellenes, *Bruchstücke zur nähern Kenntniß des heutigen Griechenlands gesammelt auf einer Reise von J. L. S. Bartholdy im Jahre 1805-4*, (1805) which also appeared in French as *Voyage en Grèce fait dans les années 1805-4*. (1807) Another historical persona that appears in the novel is Adamantios Koraes (1748–1833), a towering figure of the Greek Enlightenment. However, an actual meeting between the two historical figures is not recorded. In addition, there is mention of Samuel Hahnemann (1755–1843), the German physician and founder of 'homoeopathy,' Queen Pomare IV of Haiti (1813–1877) and the Swiss philosopher Jean Jacques Rousseau (1712–1778).

It is the weaving of places familiar to the picaresque genre, namely, Greece and the Mediterranean, with remote and exotic places that makes this novel so deliciously outlandish. An example of this is the scene where Xouth, exiled into the wilderness of New Orleans, dismisses Rousseau's view that people could live in solitude.

In New York, Anaxagoras Ligarides—Xouth's new master and pompous nephew of Old Maloukatos—finds Marietta, his cousin and the lost daughter of the latter, initially from Chios. In Egypt, the adherents of the homoeopathic school of the German physician Hahnemann enter a fistfight.

The plot starts in *medias res* as Xouth, like Odysseus, tells the story of his adventures now that his trials have seemingly come to an end—as signified, in this case, by Xouth unexpectedly regaining his human voice. He indicates to his master that his trials will soon be over, which seems to mark the plot's denouement. In addition, Xouth may have facilitated the anagnorisis of the subplot, i.e. in the story of the girl Elvira, whom the former's new master Ligarides recognises in New York as Marietta, the lost daughter of his uncle Old Maloukatos. Since Marietta is his uncle's sole heir, he tries to forestall the recognition, but Xouth witnesses all this and is very sympathetic towards Old Maloukatos. Again, we do not have the end, but it seems quite likely that Old Maloukatos eventually found his daughter with the help of Xouth.

Recent scholarship has discussed the intertextual relation of *Xouth, the Ape* to other simian literature of the time and has sought to identify the novel's place in the larger European novelistic map, as it were (Iatrou, 2017, pp. 11, 12). Panagiotis Roilos has explained how this pivotal novel engaged with the intellectual debates about the role of the novel in modern Greece and the Western perception of contemporary Greeks, and how it satirised the Greek self-perception as being the direct descendants of the ancient Greeks, between East and West; between national assertiveness and mimicry (aping) of a Western ideal of themselves (Roilos, 2003, pp. 69, 70). Pitsipios' choice to substitute an ape for a donkey in his novel was not by chance.

One peculiarity about the process of Xouth's transformation is that it is unclear whether this 'transformation is supernatural, or a mere deformation caused by his wild solitary living' (Iatrou, 2017, p. 13), i.e. whether it is an abrupt or a gradual process, respectively. In the case of the latter, Xouth differs from Lucius, who was accidentally transformed into a donkey because of his curiosity. Transformation appears to be part of the protagonist's atonement and redemption. The hero's seven-year exile into the wilderness of Louisiana after his terrible crime and his solitary confinement, wherein he constantly hears a voice, has strong Christian, biblical overtones.

Like the ancient precursors, however, our protagonist retains his human capabilities except the ability to speak, so he can observe and narrate what he has seen. However, in our novel, the internal narrator (Xouth)—unlike Lucius in *The Golden Ass*—does not tell his story merely for entertainment but rather holds a mirror into the face of his internal narratee (Evgenides). Interestingly, the first scene revolved around a mirror; this is a pivotal symbol, as the image of oneself becomes a fundamental leitmotiv of the novel.

Bartholdy is arrogant but gullible and falls prey to scheming women who take advantage of him or even cause his downfall, like Violanda, Philippina and 'Countess Avedrotte.' Evgenides is similarly manipulated by Soultana. He is vain, idle and naive.

It is not only the main story of the life of Jakob Bartholdy that is meant to open the eyes of Evgenides, but also the inset stories, the episode of Ligarides, the former master of Xouth and friend of Evgenides (another anagnorisis). Ligarides, too, is full of himself and conceited. In certain ways, Ligarides is aping Bartholdy. Like the latter, he too writes his 'oriental' travelogue, but being Greek himself, he must orientate himself further East; hence, Egypt is his suitable object. Ligarides, too, falls prey to cunning locals who charge him a fortune for their 'services,' providing him with useless material and even inscribing graffiti on important monuments on his behalf. We remember that it was widespread practice among foreigners who visited Greece, like Lord Byron, to inscribe their names on ancient monuments.

In other aspects, Ligarides is like Evgenides; both are obsessed with a European nation, the former with England and the latter with France, and each slavishly mimics his role model in every way. They each put their hopes on the foreign nation for the salvation of Hellas. They are both equally naive in political matters.

Xouth, The Ape and Polyglossia

Regarding its language, the novel is realistically 'polyglossic' in that it uses different variations of Greek spoken at the time. The protagonist and characters like Evgenides use an affected, archaic Greek, whereas non-elite characters use a colloquial form. Each language variant represents a different world, rooted in historical reality, thus creating a multi-linguistic consciousness. When the Greek state founded the 'Katharevousa,' this 'purifying language' was established as the official language of the administration and the military and was used in education. This language was a construct based on the Greek used by the Eastern Church and went back to Anna Komnena, the second sophistic and, ultimately, the classical Greek canon. The Katharevousa aimed to 'cleanse' the Greek nation from all vestiges of foreignness, especially Turkish and other Eastern influences, and to connect modern

Greece with its ancient past. In Germany, Herder first discussed the importance of language for establishing a national identity in his concept of 'Volkssprache.' Koraes, again, was instrumental in the creation of the Katharevousa, which was attacked for being far removed from Greek reality. The 'question of language' was to become an object of fierce controversy between right- and left-wing politics, conservatives and liberals, up to the 1980s.

In the novel, the main characters use the Katharevousa to be in tune with the latest fashion. The mysterious and demi-mondaine Soultana can use both the Katharevousa and her own dialect. Minor characters who are not elites, like Sultana's maid, Ploumou, as well as Don Giurumis and his family, speak the Franco-Smyrniac variant. Interestingly, they are simple but quite dexterous, cunning but not malicious. Ploumou is a simpleton, but her questions are striking in all their naivety. She asks her mistress with unabashed and refreshing honesty, 'Why do you pretend to love somebody whom you don't?' and 'Why do you want to wear your hair in the same way as a French murderess, just because she is Parisian and fashionable?'

The Portrayal of the Other

The novel is also riveting for its portrayal of Jewish people. It is the first Greek novel with an awareness of the Jewish community in Greece. The tone is antisemitic, and Jews are typecast, but we must also remember that the protagonist (internal narrator) is unreliable. He is a murderer and has lived a life of vice and debauchery. How seriously can we take his judgment of people? Jewish characters are indeed associated with cunning and businesslike acumen in this work. Don Giurumis, who exploits Bartholdy, is Jewish, as are the 'Countess Avendrote,' the crook who pretends to be Bartholdy's sister and the contractors who exploit Ligarides. But we must be careful not to jump to conclusions since Christians are also portrayed in that way (Ligarides, Don Giurumis).

Equally, it could be argued that the book is misogynistic because of the way it portrays women. All women (Philippina, Countess Avendrote, Soultana, Violanda) are represented as scheming, manipulative and downright wicked. However, we must bear in mind that men are not put in a better light.

In conclusion, the book's overarching theme is the representation of the 'other' and the difficulties this entails. *Xouth* does not have all the answers. Still, Pitsipios' complex narrative strategies, dialectical structure and satirical tone are likely intended to make his compatriots aware of these issues and heighten their critical perception. The perceptive readers of this amusing novel eventually see themselves in an unsparing mirror.

1. Kallistratos Evgenides and *Xouth, the Ape*

Kallistratos Evgenides, a freedom fighter and financier, prided himself on being the wealthiest, the most ingenious, most learned and most noble youth in Athens. He returned to Greece after his long and splendid travels through Europe in 1844. In the Enlightened Continent, he had swiftly acquired knowledge about all philological, philosophical, scientific and political matters. He had immersed himself in the fine arts and had even found time to study many old and new languages.

Kallistratos now lived in the capital of Greece, near Constitution Square and the Royal Palace. He was biding his time until his inevitable call to put his substantial knowledge, excellent virtues and tremendous experience into the service of his compatriots, his nation, the Orient, the Occident and humanity at large.

During his sojourn in England, he had bought a clever ape of the orangutan species, who went by the name of Xouth. The first master of Xouth, one of that country's wealthiest and proudest lords, had domesticated the animal to use it as a butler in the English manner. He could communicate with it merely through signs, as His Lordship loathed the idea of verbally addressing the beast like his human servants.

However, one day in August, this nobleman entered a bet with a befriended earl. He wagered that 28 November would be a dry day in London, but, alas, he was proven wrong, for on 28 November, it poured. Therefore, His Lordship, unable to bear the shame of his defeat and having to pay the earl ten pounds sterling, hung himself on the same night from one of his bedposts. This is how Xouth, the butler, was sold at an auction with the entire estate of the deceased and became the property of our most noble countryman.

   https://doi.org/10.11647/OBP.0493.01

Orangutans generally stand out among all the species of apes for their resemblance to humans; however, this similarity was even more striking in the case of Xouth on account of his frame, intellectual abilities and dexterity.

Xouth was always clad in a long suit, wore sandals and carried a small felt hat on his unsightly head. Were it not for his hirsute and wrinkled face, hairy hands with sharp nails, and speechless voice, he could have been mistaken for one of our kind.

But since we have dwelt so much on Xouth, the Ape, it would seem unfair not to say something about the noble lineage of his master, especially since the family tree of Kallistratos was by no means taller or more densely branched out than that of Xouth. Kallistratos' father was merely a humble farmer from Phrygia in Asia Minor, known there simply as Yiannis, the farmer from Phrygia.

However, ever since that humble peasant had unexpectedly acquired wealth beyond his wildest dreams during the Greek Revolution, he could afford to send his only son, Colias, to Europe to turn him into a refined and enlightened gentleman. Sadly, however, only two months after Colias' return to Athens, Yiannis died, leaving his offspring heir to a substantial fortune in money and land.

During his sojourn through Europe, Colias, the son of Yiannis the farmer from Phrygia, considered it fitting to strive towards a certain degree of elegance. Hence, Colias became Kallistratos; Yiannis became Evgenides; the 'farmer' became a 'freedom fighter;' 'Phrygian' became a 'financier.' And so, the young man ingeniously fashioned his venerable name: *Kallistratos Evgenides, Freedom Fighter and Financier*, a name under which he became known even beyond the realm of Hellas. Moreover, under this name, all the newspapers praised his rare ancestral virtues as long as he paid thirty drachmas per sentence and renewed his six-month subscription.

So, our hero, having been educated in the enlightened continent of Europe, carrying a handsome, noble and heroic name and spending his late father's money lavishly, was accepted into the highest circles of Athens with open arms.

He was present at all royal balls and received invitations to all diplomatic dinners held by ministers and foreign ambassadors. All senior diplomats in Athens, especially the European ones, admired his wit and his unrivalled knowledge, as well as the nobility of his comportment and, therefore, they added to his long-drawn name the suffix '*Le génie Grec.*'

Indeed, there was no European custom or fashion that he was not prompt in following—and, one might add, to perfection. Every tailor, shoemaker, barber, milliner and seamstress in Athens would line up, right and left of the road, whenever this *eminence grise* of Western fashion stepped out on the streets, to study him carefully from head to toe: to observe, even sniff him and then arrange their designs accordingly.

Kallistratos was unanimously elected *Protector of the Theatre, President of the Philharmonic Society, Ephor of the Club, Arbitrator of the Hippodrome, Regulator of Public Celebrations* and *Doyen General and Organiser of all Balls of the Capital*.

One could not without merit compare Kallistratos with a moral *cure-môle* sent to Greece by the beauty-loving West, with the sole purpose of freeing this hallowed ground from even the tiniest speck of primitivism, which the trustees of the national loans—in their efforts to Europeanise and civilise the barbarous Greeks with their uncouth ways—did not already succeed in erasing.

The decoration of the house of Kallistratos emulated the houses of noble young heirs of the Western world, down to its last detail. The entrance hall displayed French settees upholstered in silk, American wicker chairs, English mirrors and Moroccan tapestries. The room's centrepiece was a round table of beautiful Carrara marble, and on top of it towered a gilded Persian pipe made of Chinese porcelain, like a pyramid.

In the eastern part of this mausoleum, one could find various gilded books in Chinese, Sanskrit, Mongolian and Burmese—books that were always handy for reading and entertaining guests during Kallistratos' evening soirées. A large painting, about five feet tall and seven feet wide, was hanging opposite the grand entrance. The picture was painted in vivid colours and showed a tall man wearing a most elaborately pleated *fustanella*[1] and displaying the golden epaulettes of a European commander-in-chief while his chest was covered with European medals of honour.

---

1   *Fustanella* was the Greek traditional garment worn by the klephts and the armatoles, Greek freedom fighters. After Greece gained independence, it became the national costume of the Hellenic state.

The hero thus depicted held the scimitar in his right hand as he slayed the Ottomans, whose corpses were lying in front of his feet. With his left hand, he appeared to fasten the Greek flag in blue and white on a tower. Under the painting, one could find the following inscription in gilded letters: *The Hero, my Father, Raising the Greek Flag on the Tower of Thermopylae, Commanded by His Majesty the King of the Hellenes, on the First Month of the First Year of the Revolution.*

Next to this picture hung another, smaller one, showing a noblewoman dressed most splendidly after the European fashion and reclining on a throne embroidered with gilded threads. The figure was immersed in her book. The inscription underneath read: *Descended from the Imperial House of Constantine Porphyrogennetos, my Mother, Reading the Story of Napoleon, from the Book of her Cousin, the Duchess Abrantès.*

Various other richly gilded paintings, depicting the most miraculous events of *A Thousand and One Nights* and *Don Quixote*, covered the walls of a hall painted in the colours of the French flag, for (we reveal this on the side) this young man had a fondness for everything French, loving especially the French penchant for colourfulness.

The study featured a spectacular library that contained a miscellany of gilded books. Among the beautiful shelves of that library, we could find a particular shelf that Kallistratos had bought at a Parisian auction. It once belonged to a bankrupt merchant and was made of white ebony with a big, gilded inscription, held by two figures in relief, Hermes and Poseidon. Here, the inscription read thus: *Private Interests and Accounts*; and underneath, *Of Kallistratos Evgenides, Son of a Freedom Fighter and a Financier by the Grace of God.* On this beautiful shelf, he put only books on high diplomacy, which he had ordered from various booksellers near the Pont Neuf in Paris.

But, alas, the shipment with the various books had been dispatched before a second letter by Kallistratos—in which he had specified the exact measurements of the books—could reach the bookseller. Because of this misunderstanding, the shelves of that elegant French bookcase proved far too small. Kallistratos solved this problem by commissioning a skilled craftsman to cut the books to size. Whatever fell on the cutting floor, he placed in another elegant bookcase, on which he attached the inscription: *Remains of Antiquity.*

Near this antique bookcase, one could find other precious antiquities, such as the 'Monocle of Homer,' 'The Snuffbox of Socrates,' 'The Epaulettes of Phokion,' 'The Pipe of Peisistratus,' 'The Shoes of Diogenes,' and many more that he had meticulously assembled during his stay in Europe, following the fashionable antiquarianism.

The morning room, where he groomed himself, was also magnificent. There were four larger-than-life mirrors on the walls. In front of each mirror was a marble-topped console. Standing on these consoles were statuettes of Aphrodite, Pan and Priapus, as well as clay figurines of monkeys, cats, gargoyles and flowerpots, and a large collection of bottles filled with the finest Italian and French perfumes. A beautiful chest containing his clothes was in each of the room's four corners. On a slight elevation, in the middle of the room, was a basin where he would wash and preen himself. Under the basin stood chests containing scissors, towels, combs, pins, ear cleaners, nail polish, pinchers, boxes, bowls, soap, lotions, toothbrushes, grain, clay, perfumes and, in addition to everything else, two old razors lying on a little red square pillow interspersed with golden, gauze-like silk fabric. He showed these razors to every guest, claiming that they were the razor blades which the great conqueror of the world, Alexander of Makedon, used to shave with. He had managed to obtain these in Paris for a meagre 10,000 francs but would never agree to sell them, not for all the gold in the world, so precious were they.

The bedroom, the dining room and the remaining rooms of the house, or rather palace, were decorated with equal splendour, displaying great European refinement, yet not unmixed with certain elements and influences of Kallistratos' old country which the refined Europeans were eager to emulate. It was a perfect example of their so-called 'Orientalism,' a harmonious and dexterous weaving of such monstrously disparate worlds.

Kallistratos followed a strict regime in his daily life, as was customary for a European youth of noble extraction. Having risen at nine, he would rush to the portrait of his father and pay his respects by reaching for his hand on the canvas. Then, Xouth, together with the rest of the servants, having bowed and curtsied before the portrait and having made the sign of the cross, also kissed the foot of the pre-eminent hero of Greece before moving on to the portrait of the glorious daughter of the Porphyrogenniti.

After this ritual, the servants would silently go about their business. Kallistratos, accompanied only by his butler, would enter his toiletry room, where he would shave with the famous razor blades of Alexander the Great. He would wash his face, clean his nails, brush his teeth and pluck out any unwanted hair from his forehead and nose with silver pincers before lathering his head with scented ointments. During the entire procedure, which often lasted until noon, Xouth was on his knees, holding everything in his hands and reaching towards his master with a towel or ointment, as needed.

After this routine, he would go into the dining room, where he enjoyed a 'post-grooming breakfast.' After its enjoyment, he would leave his house in his magnificent coach—which was adorned with the family's coat of arms and manned by two servants, one of whom wore the uniform of the 'Captain of the Phallanx' and the other a gilded uniform of a European servant—and would set out to visit ministers and European ambassadors.

He would discuss all matters pertaining to the nation's significant interests with them. Later, he would drive towards Aeolos Street, where the beautiful little Soultana, the Queen of his heart, lived with her noble family. There, he would stay until four o'clock in the afternoon and relate to her everything he had deliberated with the ministers and the foreign ambassadors. Having pondered everything in his mind, he would receive her guidance about Hellas' promising future.

Back home, he would enter the toiletry room again, where he would perform the so-called 'lunchtime grooming,' and then he would have lunch with his friends if he was not by chance invited by some European ambassador.

After the meal, Kallistratos usually chatted with friends. Then, he went into his study, where he would lean back in his armchair, smoking a long pipe, and would start to listen to his secretary: the French nobleman Marquis de la Tourne-Broche, who stood to attention while reading out documents and letters until Kallistratos fell asleep and the ever-present head butler, Xouth, made a clear sign for him to stop. Then, the secretary would hand over all documents to the ape—read as well as unread—and would leave the room quietly.

Meanwhile, Xouth would collect all the documents, wrap them up, close the door of Kallistratos' room and bring them into the kitchen where, following the master's strict orders, everything had to be burned to ensure that the privacy of such a great man was protected. However, beguiled by the intoxicating smell of the freshly prepared food, the ape, instead of burning the documents, would hand them over to the Spanish sous-chef, Las Marillas, in exchange for a plate of food, which he would relish in tranquillity in the villa's garden.

The sous-chef, who considered it a sin to burn so much paper so often, sold the documents to the grocers for sixty pence per ounce. Meanwhile, Xouth, having finished his meal, would return and stand erect outside the door of his master's study with his eyes fixed on the big clock just opposite. On the eighth hour, he would enter immediately and wake up his master.

Kallistratos would now shave and dedicate himself to his 'afternoon grooming.' As soon as he had finished that task, he would come down and enter his carriage for an evening with an ambassador or with his darling little Soultana until two or three o'clock in the morning. Then, he would go to bed and sleep soundly until the following day. In short, this was approximately the daily routine of the political and social life of the smartest of all the youths of Athens.

However, one day, while Kallistratos was out, the ape, being alone in the house—nobody knows what came into his head to this day—conceived the strange idea that he, too, should shave his face. So, Xouth, having already put on the gilded and embroidered towel which the beautiful little Soultana embroidered for Kallistratos, took the hallowed blades of Alexander the Great into his hands and set to task while seeing his image in the mirror opposite the door.

But, either because of the ape's clumsiness, or because its hair was so thick, or perhaps even because the blades were accustomed to shaving only great men, Xouth could not work with them. Therefore, he put one blade between his teeth and began to try his luck with the other one.

But the moment Xouth, still dismayed with the failure of his second attempt too, was about to apply the other blade, the door suddenly burst open, and the shape of Kallistratos appeared in the opposite mirror. The sudden apparition of Kallistratos terrified Xouth so much that he let both blades slip and smash on the floor.

Kallistratos shrank with horror, seeing the priceless treasure reduced to shards. Even if the whole of Hellas, or even Europe, had been turned into ashes or deluged, he would not have felt such inconsolable and raving grief. Such was his rage that he snatched the ape by the foot, hurled him through the air and threw him to the ground—for the sybaritic European lifestyle had not yet entirely softened the natural hardiness of Yiannis the farmer's son. Kallistratos kicked him until the embroidered cloth got entangled around the ape's feet and was shredded into a thousand pieces, mired in the ape's blood.

The undignified demise of this splendid artefact of the beautiful darling Sultana enraged Kallistratos even more, adding oil to the fire. While the savagely maltreated ape settled into a corner, Kallistratos grabbed a stick and struck the wretched creature anew. Only when his victim was half-dead and he became exhausted with agony and rage did he let himself sink into the nearby armchair, where he remained numb and motionless for half an hour.

But as soon as he felt that he had regained his former strength, he snatched the sword that was hanging on the wall and charged toward the hapless ape, ready to kill it. However, at the very moment Kallistratos drew the sword, Xouth stood up on his feet and said,

'Halt, you foolish and imbecilic youth: as my master, you were entitled to hit me, and though you made more than generous use of your prerogative, you are not granted the right to go further, nor are you allowed to slaughter me.'

Kallistratos was thunderstruck when he heard the ape speaking with a human voice. The sword fell out of his hands, and he fell back into his armchair, trembling with his gaze fixed upon his interlocutor. The animal stood attentively in the opposite corner, dressing its wound with the shreds of the beautiful cloth, which he let fall with contempt. A deep silence now reigned in the hall, which Kallistratos broke first once he had composed himself.

'How is it possible that you, a dumb beast with neither feelings nor senses, without the gifts of speech and articulation, can address me now with a human tongue? Or are you perhaps some chthonic demon in the guise of a monkey?'

'Not at all,' Xouth replied earnestly, shaking his head. 'Neither am I a demon nor a creature deprived of senses and feelings, as you deem me to be. However, I wish to impart to you who I am and why I find myself in the shape of an ape and in servitude to Your Lordship. But on the morrow, since my story shall be long and important. Now we both need a good rest! Your Lordship needs to recover from the shock, and I, for my part, need to dress and nurse the injuries that Your Lordship brought upon me most unjustly. But know this, my lord: these very wounds of mine are the starting point for you and your ilk to come to their senses, whereas, for me, they are the harbingers of the swift end of my ordeal. Therefore, I urge my Lordship, as it is to your greatest benefit, not to share your consternation and astonishment about today's revelation with anybody.'

Having spoken thus, Xouth left the room with a serious mien, leaving the baffled Kallistratos numb.

(To be continued.)

2. The Journey

The following morning at nine o'clock, Xouth entered his master's room and said, 'I came, sir, to fulfil yesterday's promise. But before I begin, I entreat you to promise me that you will retain stoic calm and Pythagorean discretion no matter what will come out of my mouth. Otherwise, my narration will not only be futile; it will prove detrimental. If you cannot promise this, my lord, please command me to remain silent.'

'On the contrary,' Kallistratos answered, 'I wish you to speak, and I command you to speak openly and from your heart. I pledge to listen to you with the utmost composure and not to divulge a single detail. For this, I take an oath on the sacred remains of my heroic father.'

Upon hearing this, Xouth smiled and nodded with satisfaction.

I was born in Berlin, the capital of Prussia. My name is Bartholdy, and I am the German traveller mentioned by Adamantios Koraes in his *Prologue.* I am the unapologetic accuser of the Hellenes, the author of the book *Treatise on the More Accurate Knowledge of Modern Hellas*, published in 1805. That is who I am!

Having read as a young man the writings of various European travellers who had visited Greece, Turkey and Russia, I always burned with a desire to become myself an observer of all those miraculous things and to enter into the pantheon of the glorious explorers of the barbaric nations of the East.

My father died in 1803 and made me an heir to a large fortune that I had deposited in various banks in the German countries. Naturally, all banks gave me trust notes for every part of Turkey and letters of reference for every consul of sundry European nations. With all that in my bags, I set out first to Trieste and, from there, embarked on a merchant ship for Smyrna.

©2025 Pitsipios (text)
Christodoulides (trans. & notes), CC BY 4.0

https://doi.org/10.11647/OBP.0493.02

Upon arriving in that city, I presented myself to the consul of Austria, to whom a banker from Vienna had introduced me. This gentleman received me cordially and called upon Aggeretus, his interpreter, with whom he had a short interview, before turning back to me and saying, 'Sir, since there are no respectable hotels around, my interpreter agreed to welcome you into his house, where you will not miss any comfort, I assure you.'

So, I moved into the house of Aggeretus and his family, that is, his wife Peppa and their only daughter Violanda, the matron's brother and priest of the Capuchin order Don Giurumis, as well as one manservant and one maid.

But it was the daughter who captured my heart, and this was more so when I realised that Aggeretus' daughter displayed an equal fondness towards me. In her presence, I felt a warmth I had never felt before, especially since women usually do not notice me on account, perhaps, of my somehow unbecoming appearance and relatively small and disfigured frame.

As a matter of course, I became utterly smitten with love for sweet Violanda, quickly losing sight of everything else. Now, all my attention was devoted to making myself dashing and witty, guessing all her whims and inclinations so that I could arrange all my actions and words for her pleasure.

Since it was already spring, the family planned to move to the village of Vournova and suggested I come with them. I protested that for my travel, it was imperative that I stay in Smyrna so I could set out immediately, and that I also had to travel to the islands of the Aegean Sea, where I had to go if I wanted to gather the material necessary for the writing of my travelogue.

But Madame Peppa would have none of it, and in her Franco-Smyrniac dialect, she protested, 'Gesus Maria, what is it about all the viagattori of toute la Francia? As soon as zey arrive at Smyrna, zey commissioned Don Giurumis with all zeir business, and Avraamatsos, the janitor of ze Consulate Imperial and sent their men all over the Aegean to collect all curiosities and antiquities of old.'

And though I neither clearly understood the woman's awkward tongue nor was I convinced by her arguments, I gave in for the sake of the lovely Violanda, whose sensuous gaze carried the strongest allure possible. She convinced me that it was best to delegate my project to the Capuchin monk and Avraamatsos, a Jewish contact to the Imperial Austrian Consulate, and follow the Aggeretus family to the village of Vournova without hesitation.

After four months of living sybaritically, I returned with the family of Aggeretus to Smyrna, where Don Giurumis and Avraamatsos furnished me with a plethora of manuscripts and strange artefacts and also handed me the bill for the expenses. It was a receipt for 2,000 silver florins, of which 4,500 destilia were already paid to them in advance by the Austrian consul, as per my strict instructions.

Added to the said sum were the exorbitant expenses of the family of Aggeretus, who continued to live most lavishly after their return to Smyrna. Then, there were the lavish gifts that I bestowed on the lovely Violanda daily and the continuous purchases of new manuscripts, strange artefacts, and essential material for completing my precious oeuvre. Therefore, my resources soon dried, forcing me to turn to short-term loans.

I ended up pressed by my usurers, despised by the family of Aggeretus, and now the beautiful Violanda seemed to have lost all her interest in me. In this situation, I saw no other escape than to embark on an Austrian ship one night without a ticket and to return to Trieste. From there, I went back to my hometown, Berlin. However, since I still had the memory of the artefacts I had bought in Smyrna impressed on my mind, I decided to grace myself with the laurels of other travellers. I wrote down and published my travelogue per the habitual practice of travellers, namely, by describing the customs and morals of modern Greeks.

I wrote down the conversations I had with the so-called wise men and the prominent burghers of the towns and villages, as well as of all the cities and islands of Greece and Turkey, which I claimed to have visited. Of course, I had only seen the city of Smyrna and the village of Vournova with my own eyes. I had only made the acquaintance of the Austrian consul, of Aggeretus, of Peppa, of Don Giurumis, of Avraamatsos and their two servants, Maro and Mikhalis, and a few Jewish usurers and of course, most importantly, of Violanda.

My work was universally admired and acclaimed by all wise men and diplomats in Europe, except for a few who knew better. One day in the year 1823, as I was sojourning in Paris, it came to my attention that an old Greek man called Koraes, who had lived in that city for a long time, had mentioned my opus in his writings. He had denigrated, together with my person, to the utmost, calling me blind, stupid, silly, foolish, and my writing a shameless insult to the Greek nation.

And whereas my sycophants were utterly ignorant about me and my writing and were not in a position to pass judgment, as critics rarely are, I knew precisely both my sources and the events in Smyrna and should have, with hindsight, been more prudent and humbler. But the opposite happened; having grown more arrogant on account of the exalted reception of my work, a reception that defied every expectation, I convinced myself of the truth of the falsehoods I had written. An almost frenzied mania seized me.

So, I searched for, and found, the libellous publication of Koraes where I read his comments on me in the first volume of his *Prolegomena to Plutarch*. Incensed with rage and craving for atonement, I hastened the following morning to find this impudent little Greekling, who dared vilify my wise work and presumed to place the savage tribes of the East on an equal footing with the civilised nations of Europe.

Having found out that this man lived close to the Palais de Luxembourg, I knocked on his door at approximately ten o'clock in the morning. I entered and saw a man in his sixties sitting at a desk, surrounded by his books and writing.

'What does m'sieur want?' he asked in a friendly manner.

'To speak to a gentleman called Koraes, m'sieur!' I said curtly.

'Himself,' the old man calmly replied. 'Please, m'sieur, be seated. How can I be of assistance?'

'In no way at all, I am afraid,' I replied haughtily. 'I only came here to extract an official apology for your shameless insults.'

'I am not in the habit, m'sieur, of insulting anyone!' the old man replied, maintaining his composure. 'But how do you call yourself, m'sieur?'

'I am the traveller Bartholdy,' I replied proudly, 'about whom you surely remember you wrote in your *Prolegomena*.'

The old man was still not to be moved, but now gave me a frosty gaze mixed with contempt and anger. 'And what kind of remedy would you desire from me, M'sieur Bartholdy?' he asked, his voice now betraying an ironic undertone.

'A duel, either by gun or sword: it is of no difference to me, as I am equally fit in all kinds of duels,' I replied angrily.

'But I,' he retorted in his habitual calm, 'either through bad luck or good fortune, am neither versed in the art of the sword nor in that of the gun, nor any other weapon for that matter. Even if I were able to handle them, I would have used them only to defend my country. Surely not to furnish proof for a certain literary or political truth, a quest for which our most wise Lord has bestowed upon man the gift of speech and thought, the noblest weapons any sensible man can possess.

'So, if it pleases you, m'sieur, I am prepared to offer you a most detailed verbal defence on account of everything I have written about you and your people.

'Further, I will demonstrate that you were deceived in your opinions about the Hellenic people and will prove that as a European, you are most unjust in opening the wounds of a nation to which you owe the spiritual lights you now claim as your own. If this proposal does not seem agreeable, then good day to you, sir.'

The old man's last words somehow managed to enrage my reckless egotism even more. But, suddenly, a peculiar, most crucial sight drew my attention—a sight that restrained the rascal in me. Behind the old man, in front of a small desk, sat a young man of about twenty-five years of age whose proud and earnest demeanour, statuesque frame, large head and sinuous arms convinced me that he was an able descendant of the fabled Hercules.

As soon as I set my eyes on him, I noticed the bellicose twitching of his thick eyebrows. His fiery gaze almost made my blood freeze and instilled in me such horror that my knees began to weaken. I now remembered the story of a Frenchman, a first-hand witness of the Greek liberation struggle, who claimed that the Greek guerrillas were never in need of regular food rations because the Greeks were in the habit of eating Turks, whom they gobbled down alive, as Kronus once did with his children. So, even without the proposal of Koraes, the sight of this youth sufficiently convinced me that our differences were best settled with words only. Because, although my opponent at the duel was a weak old man, he had behind him a scribe descending from Hercules, a countryman of those who devour raw human flesh, and who, moreover, did not seem to share Koraes' stoicism and equanimity. Therefore, I replied that my honour did not permit me to insist on a duel with a weak old man and that I agreed to the proposal for a debate.

So, M'sieur Koraes started to compare the Europeans with the Greeks regarding their intellectual capacities, customs, morals, religious superstitions and social and moral virtues. He went on about the current political situation and its shining lights.

After such eloquent and unpretentious rhetoric, and after so many historical examples and illustrations, every sensible and unbiased human being, having heard this sweet-tongued old man, would have been convinced on the spot that, while we Europeans have enjoyed for centuries our civic rights and have made progress in all matters of learning, we are still not superior to the Greeks in our moral and social virtues.

Moreover, the common people of Europe have many more—and much sillier—superstitions and prejudices than the Hellenes of today. Finally, numerous European travellers to Greece take the trials and tribulations of other travellers as their sole guide. They simply carry away artefacts and other pieces, haphazardly and randomly, like mice and bees, and write about them frivolously. At other times, they rather prefer to give themselves over to a dissolute and hedonistic lifestyle, content with simply copying the writings of their predecessors, which they, in turn, publish as their own. Those travellers are imbecilic, apish creatures, unscrupulous destroyers of enlightened scholarship.

But I, still prejudiced by my egotism and having been filled with vain airs by my even more foolish acolytes, although deep down convinced by the wise words and the compelling arguments of the old man, rested my case only out of fear of the son of Hercules sitting behind him, and so I left him, glumly and lost in thought, as ignorant as I came.

3. The Recognition

Towards the evening of the same day, a tall young man, wearing a gilded uniform of a servant with a pillbox decorated with colourful feathers, came into my chambers, bowed deeply and announced that his mistress—the Countess Avendrote, a fellow German—had something important to tell me and was waiting in her carriage, in front of my hotel.

I hastened down and entered the splendid carriage of a most graceful young woman, who bade me sit next to her. This I did, greeting her with deference. Then, the manservant closed the door behind me, and the carriage started to roll for a while until it stopped in front of a stately mansion. We walked up to the house and entered a lavishly decorated hall where the countess bade me stay and sit down. I sat on a luxurious sofa, and after a short while, the countess came and sat next to me.

'You don't know me, M'sieur Bartholdy?' she asked.

'No, my lady,' I replied. 'But your servant acquainted me with the fact that I have the honour to address Her Ladyship, the Countess Avendrote.'

'More precisely,' the matron corrected with a sigh, 'with the Dowager Countess Avendrote, for it has been almost two years since Divine Providence deemed it fit to take away my consort; God bless his soul.' Upon hearing this, I whispered the usual words of comfort. 'But,' the widow went on, 'you will be surprised, m'sieur, to find out with whom you are talking and what close tie of kinship yokes us together. For when our father, many years ago (as you well know), lost his first wife, your mother, he fell in love with a young girl of humble circumstances called Caroline, whom he secretly married in 1796 because he believed he would compromise his position if he made his marriage public. I am the only offspring of that marriage.

'Sadly, six months after my birth, my mother died of a broken heart, realising that my father insisted on keeping their marriage secret.

https://doi.org/10.11647/OBP.0493.03

'His behaviour in that matter was perhaps somehow excusable because of his deference towards the social order, yet the subsequent neglect of his very own daughter demonstrated sheer callousness for having left me, after the death of my mother, with a peasant woman who lived on the outskirts of Berlin. He certainly cared for my upbringing and education and was also in the habit of visiting me in my humble dwellings, but he made no provision for me in his last will.

'Thus, after his death, I was left entirely destitute and without a guardian at the age of barely seven. Thankfully, Divine Providence, the Protectrix of the Orphans, did not abandon me, for after almost two years, a noble gentlewoman with no issue of her own took me in, and I moved with her to Vienna. She adopted me, and when she died in 1815, she made me the sole heir to her substantial fortune. In 1819, I married the wealthy Count Avendrotus, to whom I bore a son, whom I also lost three months after the passing of my husband.

'So, I am your sister by the same father, Wilhelmine Bartholdy! I have been searching for you for many years. I was told that you were travelling far away until, by chance, I noticed your wise book and immediately set out to discover your whereabouts to be close to you. The pleasure I already feel now seems to me more precious than the immensurable, but equally useless, wealth that both my guardian and my late husband have left me.'

And speaking thus, she fell round my neck and embraced me while her tender tears dropped upon me. Surprise, joy and feelings of all kinds took hold of my heart at that moment, and I embraced my only sister, unable to utter one word. We mingled our tears, and I was ecstatic with joy.

Finally, our tears drained, and we started to talk about our late father and sundry family matters. Eventually, my sister turned the conversation to my travelogue, a copy of which she had been keeping under her pillow and which she praised with so much acumen and common sense that I, still tormented by all the erudite comments of Old Koraes, brimmed with brotherly love.

At about ten o'clock, a servant announced that dinner was ready, and my sister, the countess, having taken my arm with a hand whiter than milk, led me into the second and equally luxurious hall where we sat at a lavishly laid table.

After dinner, my sister bade the servants leave before she resumed the conversation. 'Dear brother, the Lord willed it for me to remain a widow at such a young age and to take from me my sole consolation on Earth, my only son, leaving me alone with my immeasurable, but equally useless, wealth, whose possession rather enhanced my melancholy state instead of enlivening it. Deprived of all that man holds as precious, being an orphan, a widow and childless, never again allowed to enter into wedlock since I had sworn to my late husband never to marry again, I believed for a long time that I was alone in this world and would remain miserable until my last day.

'But, you see, Divine Providence seems to have taken pity on my wretched state and granted me the joy of my dear sibling. Oh, my dear brother, I hope we will never be apart from now on. In the future, I wish us to live together, and if this humble abode, which I have been living in for two years now, is not to your taste, you may buy the most splendid house in Paris or wherever it pleases you. I have a fortune of ten million francs, of which you will now be the trustee, to dispose of as you please.'

After her speech, I thanked my sister sincerely and opened my heart to her. I spoke candidly about everything that had occurred up to when I met Violanda, who was responsible for losing a great part of my fortune. I only held back the truth about my journeys and the scene with M. Koraes, and this I did only lest I offend my darling sister's decent and sensitive soul. Around midnight, my sister led me into a delightfully prepared bedroom and left, wishing me goodnight. Dizzy, on account of the champagne and the strange events of that day, I lay down on the soft bed and slept like a baby.

At about nine o'clock the following morning, I woke up and went into the great hall, where I found my sister sitting and reading my writings. After the usual morning compliments, Wilhelmine—that was her name—called her servant and ordered him to summon the majordomo of the house. The servant went out and came back with a rather corpulent man.

Wilhelmine pointed to me and said, 'His Lordship, my brother M'sieur Bartholdy, will be your sole master now, and his commands you will henceforth obey.'

The majordomo deeply bowed to me and withdrew again. A little later, I took the coach back to my hotel, accompanied by the young servant, settled my bill, packed my things and moved into my sister's mansion.

Once back in the house, as I was conversing with Wilhelmine, the corpulent majordomo appeared and asked me deferentially at what time my Lordship wished for breakfast to be ready. I wanted Wilhelmine's opinion, but she immediately said that this depended solely upon my whims as the master. So, I set the twelfth hour for breakfast and the fifth hour for lunch.

After breakfast, my sister told me that she wished to celebrate our reunion with a festive meal, to which she suggested I invite my Parisian friends. I approved her proposition, called the majordomo and commanded him to arrange a splendid repast for twenty people. I also discussed with him the various vintages of the finest wines. After that affair was settled, too, I decided to take an invigorating walk and to call upon some of my friends I intended to invite for dinner.

At the fourth hour, I returned to the house with a few guests, and once inside, I asked to see my sister and introduce her to them, but a servant said she had gone out shortly after me. Therefore, I asked my friends to stay in the great hall and went into my private chamber to change my shirt. But alas! I was thunderstruck to discover that my two trousseaux, which I had brought in a few hours ago from my hotel—one of which contained all my clothes and the rest of my fortune, consisting of 50,000 francs approximately, both in gold and banknotes—were now gone. My scream immediately alerted my friends and all the servants, who rushed into the room.

I cast a look at the servants, and my gaze was searching for the young servant but, being unable to spot him, I addressed the corpulent majordomo.

'Where is your mistress?' I asked.

'She has died, m'sieur!' he replied.

'What nonsense you are mumbling, stupid man?' I retorted.

'Unfortunately, I am not talking nonsense, m'sieur. My late wife passed away eight years ago, and she was buried at Versailles when...'

'Who asked you about your wife?' I interrupted with rage, 'I asked about your Mistress, the lady of this house, the Countess Avendrote.'

'I beg your pardon, m'sieur, but the Countess Avendrote is not the mistress of this house,' the corpulent man said, 'for I bought this house in a transaction duly carried out in the presence of two notaries and turned it into a hotel, since the passing of my wife forced me to leave Versailles and come to Paris. I leased this wing to you from yesterday, a suite of eight rooms with furniture, for 300 francs per day, so that you may live here with your most gracious sister. And now, may I announce lunch?'

'What?' I shouted. 'You impertinent man! This house does not belong to Countess Avendrote. Did you not tell me this yesterday? And where are my two trunks?'

'M'sieur,' the corpulent majordomo continued calmly, 'I thank you to be more reserved in your choice of words, for you speak to a French citizen who had the honour to serve in the Eighteenth Battalion of the Garde Nationale during the glorious days of the Emperor. I am a hotelier! The said mademoiselle came yesterday in a coach of your servant's and leased this dwelling in your name, Sir Bartholdy. After a while, you came with them. This morning, you called me, and in front of all the servants, you approved your sister's contract, having asked to be recognised as the only master.

'And, of course, I recognise you as my master and humbly bow in front of you. I respect you as such until you have settled the bill and departed. It was not my place to inform you when your sister took the lease, for it was your responsibility rather than mine to know these facts. Moreover, I am not accustomed to speaking about matters I am not asked about, especially since I know all too well that you grandees require us hoteliers to be prompt and discreet. And while I proudly announce that I am this kind of man, m'sieur, dinner awaits you, and it is a sin to let a dinner on which 4,000 francs were spent be eaten cold. Something that would displease me, if I may say so, as it would jeopardise the excellent reputation of my hotel.'

'To the devil with you and the reputation of your hotel's food,' I shouted, 'I was robbed, and you surely were conspiring with that wicked woman. I will go to the police immediately...'

'No, sir,' the corpulent hotelier retorted, 'not before you pay me what is due to me.' And speaking thus, he ordered his lackeys to arrest me. Meanwhile, I was about to implore my friends to go to the police in my stead, but I now realised that they had already vanished as soon as the altercation started.

Thus, the hotelier sent for a police officer, who came and listened with the most remarkable indifference to both our depositions. He estimated the hotel bill at 4565 francs and the lunch at 1900 francs. After a generous discount from the hotelier, which the police officer had insisted on, he decided that I had to pay the hotelier immediately. However, since the so-called Countess Avendrote defrauded me, I had the right to sue her following article—I know not which—of the *Code Pénal*. However, because I had not a farthing in my pocket, the hotelier demanded that I be arrested by the constable who, with great politeness, while smoking his cigarette with content, took me and locked me up in the prison of Sainte Pélagie.

4. The Release

I was incarcerated for three months in the prison of Sainte Pélagie, eating only bread and deprived of the essential comforts of life. Most regrettable of all, I could not search for my defrauder. For, as the constable told me, under the law, the further handling of the case was in the hands of the public prosecutor. I succeeded in having an interview with him when he visited the prison approximately one month after my incarceration, and I related to him the story of my unexpected misfortune.

He looked in his book and said that the following article, so-and-so—I don't remember which—required a complaint to be submitted in writing. Therefore, I bade my prison guard call a councillor so that I could set up the complaint. But the councillor asked me for twenty-five francs in advance as soon as he came, and as I did not even have twenty-five farthings, he left me, demanding two francs for the visit and threatening to take them by force, as was his right.

Therefore, I asked him to write a long and grovelling letter to the public prosecutor, who duly replied that since I had no means of paying legal and court bills, I should address myself to the mayor of my hometown and seek a 'certification of poverty.' With this, I should come to him and pledge on the Holy Bible that as soon as my financial situation improved, I would defray all my expenses, and he would do his utmost to uphold the law and public security. In conclusion, he assured me of his most profound respect and asked me not to doubt his commitment to doing everything that would help.

Three months of agony had already passed, and one morning, I saw the fat hotelier entering the visitors' room of the prison in the company of a handsome man who must have been in his fifties. As far as one could tell, the latter was certainly not one of those who had served in the Eighteenth Battalion of the Garde Nationale in the glorious days of the Emperor.

https://doi.org/10.11647/OBP.0493.04

'M'sieur Bartholdy,' the stranger said in German while coming towards me, 'I am a friend of your father's and a compatriot, living now for many years in Paris. As soon as I heard of your misfortune, I hurried to your hotel and settled the bill. This man now wants to hand you the receipt. So, if you please, as a free man, you may now follow me to my house, where you will find all necessary comforts.'

While the man spoke thus, the fat hotelier gave me the receipt of payment, which stated that M'sieur Carl Roffer paid the amounts of 4565 and 1900 francs. Having shaken my hand heartily, while his belly, his arms and his head moved towards all directions, he asked for pardon on account of his previous behaviour towards me, which, he maintained, was dictated not by avarice for such a small amount but out of a sheer sense of honesty and respect both for himself and his business.

The generosity of my paternal friend moved me to tears of boundless gratitude. And this is how it came about that I followed M'sieur Roffer into his house. But, alas, how often a most generous deed becomes the very source of the most terrible calamities and most heinous crimes.

5. The Crime

M'sieur Carl Roffer lived in the quartier of Saint Honoré, in a house that he owned, which was not grand but quite pleasant. Inside, though not decorated in the most extravagant style, it still showed that the master of the house lived in great comfort. Actually, M'sieur Carl Roffer, a merchant in diamonds for many years, was one of the wealthiest men in Paris.

Nature itself had endowed this man with the best moral qualities. His generosity, his charity, his equanimity, his uprightness, his piety, his common sense and all other virtues visibly guided all his actions.

But Fortuna, who, on the one hand, aided him in all his enterprises and made him the master of a vast estate, also visited upon him the deadliest poison known to man: Philippina, his wife. She was one of those chthonic fiends that Hades occasionally spits out of its bowels onto the Earth in the shape of a woman—a blasphemous insult to the weak gender.

This female was of a most wicked and base nature, impious, a common liar and a shameless prevaricator. She was promiscuous, tempestuous, paranoid, inhuman and deprived of any sense of humanity and honour. Sometimes a most stingy miser, at other times a most flagrant prodigal. She could, without exaggeration, be described as the bane of quietude and peace, the open wound of the sensible heart and the living death of her poor husband.

Every kind of wickedness found harbour in her poisoned soul. Any wicked deed and every crime were acceptable for her if they served her evil schemes. But worst of all, this diabolical creature seemed set upon slandering her guileless husband with all means, spreading the most outrageous rumours via a gang of depraved ruffians, men and women whom she had the unique ability to place under her spell and manipulate for her satanic schemes.

And wretched M'sieur Roffer, though he knew about her abominable crimes, corrupted lifestyle and shameless deeds, and was possessed by

https://doi.org/10.11647/OBP.0493.05

the deepest sense of honour, always tried his best to cover and hide his plight from the world. However, he sighed bitterly in secret and honestly believed—the fool—that that lost woman could be brought to her senses. There were times, though, when he only wished for his death.

And if anger against Philippina escaped from his anguished heart by chance, the next day he regretted it and tried to justify her in front of the same people to whom he had expressed his rancour, blaming only himself for her behaviour. However, his friends, who often advised him to send this woman away, were not given heed. Therefore, they despised him, calling him a senseless and foolish man. This was the kind of woman towards whom my demon directed my destructive desire.

By no means are wicked deeds always perpetrated by people who are by nature evil, nor does a man become wicked in an instant or out of a single cause. Terrible criminals are like great rivers: goaded by unbridled passions, possessing a natural weakness, misled by false ideas and burdened with a twisted mind and lack of judgment. Sloth, evil role models, wealth acquired without toil or sudden poverty, and boundless fancy and vanity are the terrible rivulets that gradually form this dreadful river.

But reason, which lingers below the violent currents of such a river, does still feel the danger, yet is laid numb by passions, aware that it cannot move as the man is chased by a heavy nightmare.

I was not born wicked. On the contrary, I had an innocent soul and a good heart, but by nature, I was a victim of my impulses, consumed by vanity. In addition, I was robbed, defrauded and the object of other people's malice. Moreover, since I had lost all my family fortune, I was constantly daydreaming about how to come again into the possession of wealth, which, so I believed, brought happiness.

Furthermore, I was not accustomed to pursuing regular work and prone to becoming the victim of hustling women. Therefore, it was only natural that I carved my ultimate destruction and, having found myself entangled in the filthy nets of that fiendish Philippina, be cajoled into committing the most atrocious of crimes.

My soul shudders with horror whenever I remember the most hateful part of my sorry tale. I will not even dare describe the details of this unspeakable deed. Alas, if only it could be eradicated from my consciousness.

The terrible upshot of this was that on 15 March 1825, Carl Roffer, being murdered, was laid to rest, whereas I, disguised as a peasant, was on my way to England with the blood of this virtuous man on my hands.'

At this point, Xouth stopped, overcome by tormenting memories, and was unable to continue his tale. But after a few minutes of silence, he continued.

6. Divine Justice

On the first night of my flight from Paris, I came to a villager's hut and spent my night in the adjacent barn. I was seized by the horror that the first perpetrated criminal act typically leaves on those not accustomed to committing wicked deeds, tormented by pangs of consciousness; I sought relief in the soothing balm of sleep.

But, as soon as I half-closed my eyelids, I was violently shaken by a loud noise. I jumped up in terror, and my eyes perceived in that dense darkness a tall ghost, a creature wrapped in a white sheet stained with spills of blood. Black signs were visible, forming the numbers 4565 and 1900. In the angry, menacingly gazing face of this gigantic skeleton, I recognised the apparition of the late Carl Roffer, still holding in his right hand my book, dripping with his blood.

'Mercy!' I exclaimed in horror. 'Please, forgive me.'

But this portent turned towards me with a loud din of clashing bones, grabbing me by the neck with its bony hand and shaking me with an inconceivable force.

'All wicked men try to find refuge in forgiveness when they see punishment approaching,' he said. 'Now, reap the fruits of your crime!'

The coldness of his steely hand froze my blood; my ears were shuddering, I lost my sight, and I fell to the ground like a corpse.

When I came back to my senses the following morning, I left this terrible abode, panic-stricken, and headed towards the city of Calais. When I arrived there, I saw some Englishmen, and from their conversation I gathered they were about to embark on a ship for America. I wanted to ask if they could take me with them, but strangely, my voice had abandoned me! So, having breathed heavily, I turned my eyes towards the sky, but then again, that terrible portent with the bloodstained sheet appeared over my head. My horror grew, and I fell to the ground again.

©2025 Pitsipios (text)
Christodoulides (trans. & notes), CC BY 4.0   https://doi.org/10.11647/OBP.0493.06

Having regained my senses, I approached the sailors and was able to communicate with signs. I embarked on a ship and sailed with them.

During the entire voyage, the frightening portent constantly appeared to me on any given occasion. Sometimes, I would see it walking on the waves of the ocean, higher than the mast of a ship; at other times, sitting next to me in the shape of the late Carl Roffer, pointing to the mysterious number on the sheet—a mirror of my dismal ingratitude towards my victim.

But especially at night, when I closed my eyelids, the skeletal, steely hand of the ghost of Carl Roffer on my neck was almost stifling me, while the terrible echo of his menacing threats and the dreadful creaking and clashing of his arid bones terrorised my ears.

Then there were times when, in my nightmares, I saw the hateful Philippina dancing shamelessly in front of me, mocking me in my agony. One day, I decided to put an end to my wretched state by throwing myself into the depths of the abyss. However, an invisible power prevented me from executing my plan whenever I set out to the task. In this state, I eventually reached New Orleans.

In vain had I hoped that in escaping the place of my crime, the change of scenery and the sight of entirely unknown and new people and places would ease my heavy conscience. Quite the opposite. Everybody in that city now appeared to me like the gory ghost of Carl Roffer. I fled from the city in panic, like a lunatic, with the haunting echo of its menacing threats and the dreadful din of the violently creaking arid bones of the ghost that was pursuing me.

After roaming countless hours, I found myself on a vast plain. Looking behind me, I saw the horrible portent of Carl Roffer again. This time, it was even taller than the highest church tower, holding the bloody sheet of paper. I mustered my strength and ran into the woods. Not knowing the road back, I had to find shelter under an old cedar. Though pressed hard by hunger and thirst and without any sign of relief, I decided to remain there until dawn.

To my surprise, the terrible monster left me in peace that night in the woods. I even felt a little calm. A deep slumber came over my weary limbs, and I slept through until the following noon. Naturally, when I woke up, I was still hungry and thirsty, and wild fruit and water from a lake visible from afar were able to satisfy my needs. For ten days, I wandered from rock to rock, from mountain to plain, from plain to desert, feeding on wild fruit, berries and verdant roots, sleeping in trees and trying in vain to find a path toward an inhabited place.

But during these difficult days, I miraculously got my morale back because I was not harassed anymore by that terrible portent.

Finally, on the eleventh day, in the morning, I perceived a distant village. I hurried towards it, but as soon as I came close, I met the terrible portent of Carl Roffer again, threatening me and waving the gory sheet with his skeletal hand. I turned back again and ran towards the wilderness, with the terrible threats and din of the clashing bones chasing me.

So, I returned to the wilderness. And there I suddenly heard a voice, like a thunderbolt, 'Thou shalt be exiled from society and mayst not be allowed to return to the company of men until you have atoned in the eyes of God and regained the gift of speech!'

Perceiving my ineluctable destiny, clearly laid in front of me, I decided, willy-nilly, to bear the just punishment of my crime and to remain in the desert. After that encounter, the dreadful sound of the vengeful threats did not torment me anymore with the hideous din of the creaking bones of the monster.

7. The Wilderness

Having roamed the wilderness for six days, seeking a suitable refuge, I finally came across the likeness of a cavernous hollow at the foot of a hill, made of a roughly hewn rock, which seemed most suitable as a dwelling. This cavity could handily protect me at night from the assault of beasts. At the same time, the rivulet running nearby and the abundance of fruit, nuts and berries from the adjacent forest could satisfy my most primal needs. Therefore, I cleared the hollow as much as I could, gathered leaves of the cane, spread them on the ground and found a square rock, which I carried towards the entrance to use as a door.

This was now my new home, and my days were consumed in dismal thoughts, which the notion of my cruel exile made vivid at every given moment. There, I felt the pressing need for self-examination, the urge to understand the principle 'Know thyself,' which every man must discover in himself, a sacred duty towards God and man alike. Having lived in that desolate place, I came to realise how much Rousseau and the other phoney philosophers were wrong in claiming that a human being can find bliss outside the society of men.

Alas, how often did those wild, high winds howl outside my desolate cave, and the howl of the wild beasts shake all my senses? The terrible clamour of the thunder seemed to me like the end of the world, and the lightning appeared to be more fearsome than the abysmal darkness of a moonless night as it flashed through the cracks of my cave that was shaking all over. How often did I long to behold a fellow human being, even if it were in the terrible form of the ghost of Carl Roffer!

And while the days and the nights passed thus (I marked every passing day at the entrance of my cave), I counted seven years in the desert. I was already accustomed to living like a wild beast but could never assuage the pain of my exile from the society of humans.

©2025 Pitsipios (text)
Christodoulides (trans. & notes), CC BY 4.0

https://doi.org/10.11647/OBP.0493.07

The clothes that I was wearing when I was exiled, torn asunder, were rags now, but my skin had become so hardy from all the trials, the heat of the sun and the onslaught of the winds that it became black and was covered by hair and a kind of fur. My countenance changed so much that my human shape became unrecognisable.

8. The Captivity

One day, it must have been around noon; as I was roaming the shady woods in search of food, I suddenly saw a pair of European shoes on the ground. Both the sight of this object in the middle of the wilderness and the pleasantly comforting idea of human company that shot through my mind like thunder made me concentrate so much on that finding that I stood for almost half an hour with my gaze fixed upon it, trying to guess where these had come from.

At the end, wearied from trying to fathom this unexpected thing, I took one and, having sat down, tried to put it on, but as soon as I put my foot into it, I immediately felt a sticky material of some sort in which my foot stuck. In panic now and trying to pull my foot out of the shoe again, I suddenly heard a clamour of a stampede, and on turning back, I saw many hunters who fell upon me with knives and guns.

'He is caught! He is caught! Beware, beware!' they shouted.

My first reaction, either out of fear of guns or of the shouts, was to run away, but I slipped and fell flat the very moment ten hunters arrived and caught me. First, they carefully cut off the shoe from my foot, which—as I inferred later from their conversation—was a trap by which the inhabitants of those regions customarily ensnare apes. The huntsmen intended to tie my arms and legs with iron chains, but, seeing that I was motionless, they considered it sufficient to merely put a collar around my neck and fasten it on a long chain by which they dragged me.

For five days, I was towed along in a state of numbness until we reached New Orleans. When I entered the city, I realised that the terrible portent of Carl Roffer had not chased me this time, but I still shuddered at the echo of its terrible words. 'Thou art exiled from the company of men and forbidden to dwell as a man in their society until atoned in the eyes of God, the Almighty, and hath regained the gift of the human tongue!' I interpreted this command thus: I was destined to live in the society of

https://doi.org/10.11647/OBP.0493.08

men, but in the form of the mute beast, and therefore I decided to accept my sentences without remonstrance, hoping only for God's mercy.

The day after we arrived in New Orleans, I was sold by my captors as a beast to a Frenchman, who took me to New York. Noticing that I was tame throughout the voyage, he removed my collar. He started to train me in various household chores, which I performed consummately, like a human being, but also with great dexterity, like an ape. On account of this, on our second day in New York, my master—having observed my remarkable resemblance to a man out of fancy—dressed me in clothes and, seeing that I was pleased with them, ordered that I be dressed henceforth in the clothes I wear to this day.

So, having resolved to behave as well as possible like the ape in whose shape I was destined to atone for my crime, I mimicked that animal in every way, taking care to display as little dexterity as possible so as not to be irked too much by the tiresome curiosity of my master and the silly pranks of a close friend of his, Anaxagoras Ligarides, who seemed the most foolish young man I have ever set eyes on. Against him, I had conceived the utmost disdain.

'Anaxagoras Ligarides!' Kallistratos cried out with the greatest surprise. 'He is a very close friend of mine! We met in Paris and had quite some fun together. Though he had the bad fortune to be the nephew, he claimed, of some boorish and stupid miser, from whom he hoped to inherit soon. His only vice is that he admires the English too much because he says they are very comely. But he is nonetheless a wise, ingenious and noble young man.'

'Whatever you say!' Xouth retorted, shaking his head. 'My misfortune was the greater, since though I had prayed from my heart often for a new master, my fate was like that of the frogs in the proverb, who had asked Zeus for a new lord! For, after six months, my lord left for England and left me with the said friend of his, Anaxagoras Ligarides, whose true character I wish to reveal to you since I see you entertain many a false impression.'

9. Ligarides

My new lord, being arrogant and egocentric as only an Englishman could be, vain as a woman and imprudent, like a moth that flies around the open flame, was always in the habit of wildly gesticulating with every word he uttered, like a retard. He would have been insufferable, even to a genuine ape. However, most of all, he was obsessed with aping the English in a way that was outright imbecilic, as he admired, in his stupidity, even the most obvious faults of those people.

In his speeches, he constantly stated that the Hellenic nation could only flourish under British influence, namely, by handing the national government into the hands of those cunning connivers whom he called 'capable and honourable.'

'Alas,' Kallistratos exclaimed in dismay, 'Ligarides always had this folly. I could never convince him that foreign interventions always lead to the undoing of a nation and that only the French influence could elevate our country to that state of prestige and glory that Hellas, among all European nations, last possessed in the time of Plutarch.'

'I see we are digressing; I will return to my story,' Xouth retorted.

So, in New York, Ligarides was instructed in law, and his wealthy uncle from the island of Chios, Zannes Maloukatos, paid for the tuition. I met his uncle sometime later in Smyrna and found him to differ markedly from the portrait of him that Ligarides painted for you.

For the old man, who—if he still lives today—must be around sixty, was pious, honourable, just and caring, humble and dignified. Moreover, what is rare among the Greeks today is that he was honest and decent. He did not champion, under the disastrously silly fashion, the interests of

©2025 Pitsipios (text)
Christodoulides (trans. & notes), CC BY 4.0

https://doi.org/10.11647/OBP.0493.09

any foreign power. Maybe his only vice worth mentioning was his great respect and deference for the old values, morals and government of Chios.

And though he had received no formal education and possessed no knowledge of Europe and its culture, he had by nature a sound mind and common sense and was considered a very wise and upright gentleman. Having lived for many years in Russia, where he was a merchant and had acquired substantial means, he now lived in retirement. He had no children. He loved Ligarides like a son and designated him as the sole heir of his considerable fortune.

It would be of no avail to narrate in detail the moral disappointments that I experienced living under the tyranny of this foolish young man. Among other things, he once wished to be painted by a famous painter in New York and paid the artist a visit one morning. However, a few hours later, about noon, I saw him rushing home in great agitation, utterly beside himself. As soon as he entered and threw his hat with rage on the table, he fell into an armchair, the picture of a man overcome by the greatest despondency.

He called his servant and instructed him to hurry and call upon his lawyer, a certain Mr Pegadostomides, also a native of Chios, who had trained as a lawyer in America before becoming acquainted with him.

The servant rushed out immediately, and Ligarides, raving mad, incessantly walked up and down the corridor, breathing heavily, leaning his head on the wall, and remaining entirely motionless. Sometimes, he leapt towards the window, looking out anxiously to see if Mr Pegadostomides was nearby. Then he would fall back into his armchair and, crossing his hands or placing his palms together, would whisper whimsically incomprehensible words, out of which I could make no sense.

Finally, Mr Pegadostomides arrived. Ligarides, as soon as he saw him, cried out loud, 'I am lost, dear friend, I am done for... help me, please!'

'What is the matter? What happened? Speak to me about it, my friend, and we may find a remedy.'

So Ligarides rushed and shut the door, placed two chairs opposite each other, asked the attorney to sit down, and began to speak. 'You know that today I intended to go to the house of the painter Jonas to sit for my portrait. I went there at nine, but as soon as I entered the painter's atelier, I saw a most becoming young woman, whom I first took for Jonas' daughter, and congratulated him on the young girl's beauty.

'She is not my daughter,' the painter replied, 'but rather a compatriot of yours who, having been captured during the Massacre of Chios when just a baby of ten months, was ransomed, together with her governess, by an American captain, who was at that time in Smyrna. He brought her to New York and, since he was a bachelor, gave her to me to raise. I brought her up in my family since her nurse had just died shortly after they were freed.

'Now, this young girl wore an amulet around her neck with a picture, a portrait of her father, as her nanny had informed the captain. Afterwards, the captain forgot the name of Elvira's father (that was her name). And we have not succeeded to this day in shedding light on any of this,' the painter concluded, turning towards the girl. 'Please, dear, show this gentleman, who is also Greek, the picture of your father.''

'Elvira immediately removed the golden chain from her neck. 'Please, sir,' she begged with a sigh.

'But what a shock when I immediately recognised the face of my uncle Maloukatos and therefore realised straight away that Elvira was, in truth, Marietta, his only born daughter and my cousin. She was captured during the destruction of Chios when she was ten months old, together with her wet nurse. I was left thunderstruck and almost gave myself away, but managed to compose myself and hide my consternation, pretending to carefully peruse the picture, and having done so, l gave it back to this 'Elvira.'

'It does not ring a bell,' I said with feigned indifference. 'I have never seen this person in my life.''

'You know well, my friend, that my uncle tried so often to find out what had happened to his only offspring, but had not succeeded in finding her and eventually was convinced that she was dead. He, therefore, appointed me recently as his sole heir. But if he finds out that Marietta is alive, I will lose my inheritance. In the name of our friendship, I beseech you to advise and help me steer clear of this calamity. Rest assured that I am prepared to reward your services most generously.'

The attorney stood up, stooped a bit, craned his neck and stared with his shifty gaze. Then he pretended to adjust his suit as if to remove the creases, swallowed a few times and finally said to his friend, 'Guided by the light of my scholarship, I am in a position to offer you many valuable means through which you could duly legitimise this inheritance that is

due to you. For one, your uncle named you heir; that decision is final
and cannot be revoked. However, it is necessary to add the clauses that,
per civil procedure, would protect your legal rights in the unexpected
event of the appearance of a third party, namely, your cousin Marietta.

'Of course, many issues are at stake here, but since Marietta is alive,
there is a real possibility that she might litigate and take away from
you—out of your very hands, so to speak—this splendid inheritance on
which all your hopes for the future rest. However, by taking it away,
Marietta becomes a secondary cause of your ultimate misfortune and,
of course, the secondary cause of misery is without the slightest doubt
an enemy: and the more so, the bigger the calamity that stems from it.'

'Now, both natural law and our penal code grant us the right to
self-defence against our enemies. Those unquestionable legal principles
are further strengthened by the theories of the great political theorist
Machiavelli, who believed that a defence must always be absolute.

'So, for all of the above, and considering your special circumstances,
I advise you to make haste and remove your cousin Marietta.'

'I do not understand, my friend,' Master Ligarides replied. 'What do
you mean by removing?'

'I mean what I just said!'

'What?'

'What?' Mr Pegadostomides repeated ironically, gesticulating with
agitation. 'Obviously, to murder her either by poison, through an
ambush or by any other means!'

Ligarides cried out in surprise, and after a few minutes of silence:
'Oh,' he said, sighing. 'I cannot do this! My conscience would always
torment me after that.'

'Ah,' the attorney at law retorted with a sardonic smile, 'what
can superstition do to a man? You are afraid of sinning, so it seems.
Conscience, my dear friend, is the weakness of petty souls, and sins are,
as I often say, merely ideas.'

At this point, Ligarides interrupted his friend. 'Enough,' he said. 'My
friend, we often spoke about these things in the past and could never
reach the same opinion. Let us leave this subject alone, and tell me if you
know of any other remedy for the present dangers.'

Mr Pegadostomides remained pensive and absorbed in these thoughts for some time before pleading his cause. 'There is no other option left for you than to marry your cousin as soon as possible.'

'You must be joking!'

'No, not at all; I am deadly serious!'

'And how am I to accomplish this in a short time? First, I am neither familiar with Marietta's nor her guardian's view on marriage. Second, I have positive knowledge that Marietta is my cousin, and our ecclesiastical and civil laws forbid marriage between close relations.'

'This is not at all difficult. You will pretend that you have fallen madly in love with her. In this way, you will win her heart and, at the same time, secure the inheritance of your uncle. As regards the prohibition of intermarriage, this is something that our ancestors may have observed, but it is out of fashion today, especially if money is involved.'

So, after some meaningless chatting, the two friends agreed, and Master Ligarides assumed the role of the love-stricken suitor of the so-called Elvira. But all his efforts were of no avail, for Elvira rejected the love of Master Ligarides with contempt, and the painter Jonas forbade him to come again into his house. While Master Ligarides was despairing, Mr Pegadostomides, after a few more attempts to convince him to murder her, took it upon himself to steal from the girl the amulet with her father's picture, to eradicate any trace that could lead to a scene of recognition between Marietta and her father.

Barely two months passed before this respectable attorney succeeded in snatching the amulet from Elvira by enlisting the services of a low-life hag for a reward of 500 talents. Mr Pegadostomides handed the picture to Master Ligarides, who paid him 100 talents for his services and the 500 to the old hag.

10. The Return

Approximately four months after the theft, Old Maloukatos wrote to his nephew and asked him to join him in Smyrna, whence he intended to invite him on a journey he was planning to undertake to the most important cities before settling in Athens, where he had resolved to spend the rest of his life. So, we embarked on a merchant's vessel to Marseille and, from there, took a French steamer and arrived in Smyrna in August 1834. But what a sight Smyrna was! Remembering my vanity and naivety in that city thirty years before, I was more ashamed about my previous follies than my present beastly state.

Old Maloukatos, having seen me, claimed that it was vanity to feed an animal that was of no use to society, and often urged Master Ligarides to give me to the pasha of Smyrna. This proposition alarmed me greatly because I knew that the pasha possessed many wild beasts, and sharing dwellings with them would certainly not be the most pleasant experience.

But either the hauteur of Master Ligarides—who attached much importance to the ownership of a rare ape—or my heightened attention in carrying out all commands of the old man during our ten-day stay in Smyrna, succeeded in convincing him to take me with him on his journeys. It even induced him to display a certain sympathy towards me.

The excellent virtues of Old Maloukatos, his daily and constant questioning of Master Ligarides about his only daughter, Marietta, and the inconsolable grief that overshadowed all his actions and words because he could not find out if she were alive or dead. All of this made me feel compelled to reveal to the old man, by any means, any secret I knew about Marietta, especially as I was party to the crime, having been able to help him but not having done so.

https://doi.org/10.11647/OBP.0493.10

So, I searched Master Ligarides' things and found the stolen amulet with the picture of Mr Maloukatos, and I placed it one morning secretly on the bedside table of the old man...'

As soon as Xouth spoke his last word, the servant of the beautiful little Soultana entered the room and asked Kallistratos to come to her house on account of a serious and most urgent matter. Kallistratos immediately ordered the coaches to be ready.

However, before we follow him into the house of the amiable young lady and find out about this matter, it is only fitting and expedient to expatiate on specific historical facts about the beautiful little Soultana and her place in Greek society.

11. The Sweet Little Soultana

The lovely Soultana, the Aspasia of modern Athens, first saw the light of this world in a seedy corner of the noble Phanar district of Constantinople—a place awash with the miraculous water of nobility, a strange natural depository of the most disparate creatures.

Having lived in Athens for roughly ten years under the respectable title of a widow, she had caught the general attention of the Athenians. Through her comeliness and allurements, she had stirred the sensible souls of several great men and glorious heroes of modern Hellas.

It is even secret knowledge that feelings for her abetted the patriotic perpetrators of the latest *coup d'état* in Athens. Thus, she helped to elevate the Greek nation to the present heights of perfection, fortune and glory. It is also claimed that from that time, the appointments of most civil servants were written upon the knees of the amiable lady, upon her dictation.

At her home, the respectable guardians of the national wealth were appointed. The senators and parliamentarians would fight and settle their differences, and the suitability of the civil servants was whetted. With one nod from the beautiful Soultana, the fugitive thief who had just escaped the prison of Medrese was appointed financial controller; the robber was promoted district officer; the unscrupulous made judge and the pimp made consul, while the malicious and depraved would become the professors of ethics and philosophy.

Moreover, in Athens, Western diplomats and their higher officers, having discovered this Pandora's box, had all rushed to turn the wheels of this maze-like machine and to gear its direction for the advantage of the ancient nation—whose resurrection and palingenesis out of the Orient both they and their governments always championed, with their accustomed sincerity and humanity.

©2025 Pitsipios (text)
Christodoulides (trans. & notes), CC BY 4.0

https://doi.org/10.11647/OBP.0493.11

Darling Soultana, having become the pivot of Greek diplomacy, the litmus test for those in charge, as well as the epicentre of the society in Athens, was justly deemed to have embodied in her person the three great powers of the Moirae of ancient mythology. The Royal Court, bowing to the indomitable flow of this political tendency, *nolens volens*, included the beautiful Soultana in the select number of invitees to the *bal de debutants*.

This was the position the delightful Soultana held in the society of Athens. As regards her private life and the nature of her relation to Kallistratos, each reader might guess for himself.

That day, inside her splendid boudoir, filled with everything that European good taste and female vanity could covet, she was lying on her sofa of purple silk—a woman of thirty years, holding a fashionable Parisian newspaper. Her morning gown, pleated and covering the floor, was made of white muslin with Valenciennes lace and bore testament to her refinement and meticulousness. The vivid movements of her big, dark eyes and her graceful gestures amply proved that she was highly versed in the craft of charming and beguiling all hearts.

Suddenly, the boudoir door opened slightly, and with the tenderness of a caring mother opening the door to the nursery of her sleeping child, the nimble parlourmaid appeared on light steps in front of her beautiful mistress.

'Missus, m'lady sent me to see if you are awake and wish to be combed.'

'I told you a thousand times, Ploumou, never to use the barbaric word 'missus!' In Constantinople, 'missus' is a gossipmonger!'

'God forbid! I would never call you a gossip; I drink water in your name.'

'I did not say you did, but I am telling you again, learn how to speak.'

'I always speak correct, m'lady, but I cannot speak fancy because they ain't sent me to school in Chios as it ain't not the custom there.'

'So, the saying that all Chiots are foolish is correct then?'

'No way, I beg you! We might not be as clever as you are, m'lady, but we ain't no stupid! You must see the lasses of Chios, m'lady! It will blow you away how much they can make; they grind barley, they can bake, and they manage to knit one sock within a day.'

'And probably they cover themselves in makeup, like witches.'

'Pardon?'

'They plaster themselves with makeup and lipstick to the extent that it becomes quite repulsive.'

'You are right, missu... eh! I mean, m'lady. Some overdo it. They walk on the promenade like the carnival troop of Karagoz!'

'But you too, m'lady, from the polite society who live in the European way, put on yourselves a thousand things. Somebody who comes into your room sees a million vessels: oils, emulsions, green and red water, and flasks, like Domenicos' Pharmacy, that is! Yours indeed smell nice, but theirs ain't bad stinking either. Indeed, those poor things don't have the bosom you have, by the mother of God. Whenever I help you with your corset, I must pull with more strength than my uncle Yiannis had to when he saddled our donkey.'

'Enough, Ploumou, I am already nauseous. I become dizzy when I hear your foolish talk. What time is it anyway?'

'Ten thirty, m'lady.'

'Good Lord. Why did you not wake me earlier, as I told you yesterday evening?'

'But, m'lady, I came into your room three times, but you snored like an angel.'

'You should have woken me, as I deliberately went to bed early.'

'Sure, but I remember you stayed up all night with the colonel spinning the wool.'

'What, colonel? You were daydreaming again?'

'Did you not hear his singing?'

'Why did you not wake me up?'

'In the middle of the night? But I did not know that you were asleep.'

'How stupid you are, Ploumou, not to wake me at the colonel's arrival.'

'That count also came yesterday at ten, what's 'is name? ...But I was ashamed to tell him you were still sleepin', so I told him you went to the theatre, and he wrote this letter here. And the soldier of the colonel also brought one, and the handsome English fella from the ship gave this to Yerasimos.'

'Let us be patient... prepare my bath, and you will comb my hair after I have it.'

'But, m'lady, how am I goin' to prepare it without any milk?'

'What? Gerasimos did not buy any today?'

'No, and the old milk started to smell like hell because it was already three days old, and your aunty... but don't punish me, m'lady, please.'

'Don't worry, just tell me the truth. So, was the milk from yesterday's bath also used for my bath two days ago?'

'Yes, because your aunty—as long as Gerasimos could resell the milk you had bathed in—always bought fresh milk for you. However, when gossip spread the word that we were selling rancid milk, not even the proprietor of the Kafenio wanted to buy it. Your Madam said that we should not buy the milk and throw it out immediately because it is a sin to throw away food. And the milk from last week, they only bought it because they found it cheap enough and used it twice for you and wanted to use it today too, but it stunk so much, and they said I should not tell it to you...'

'Enough! I see you are not the only fool in this house. Come on and comb my hair now. Look carefully at this picture, shown in this fashionable magazine, and make my *coiffe* accordingly. It is the latest fashion in Paris, according to Madame Lafarge.'

'Ooh, she is pretty, I say! But why is she in black? Did her father die?'

'No! This lady was born to aristocrats in Paris and received the best education in fashionable society. She studied music, danced charmingly, applauded gracefully in the theatre, spoke eloquently about anything, dressed elegantly and read all the novels there, from Sir Walter Scott to George Sand.

'Naturally, these novels lent wings to her imaginative disposition and led her to believe that soon she would become the wife of a *comte*, a *Ministre des Affaires Financieres*, or an *Ambassadeur en Turquie*.

'However, having been left an orphan and destitute after the death of both her parents, she had to marry a steel magnate, a man called Lafarge. He and his kin were uncouth people with no education, and they only talked about commerce and finances. Of course, with her sensible nature, this noble lady could not fit in with this vulgar lot, but as she was also clever and quite practical, she convinced her husband to designate her as the sole heir in his will.

'When this Lafarge died, the assizes sentenced this delicate creature to life in prison on the charge that she had poisoned her husband. But the graceful way she defended herself in court and the excellent manners she showed during the trial impressed the French so much that, immediately after the trial, the name 'Lafarge' became synonymous with the elegant, fashionable masterpieces of the time.'

'I say, and if she was such a bad apple, why did you fall for her, you and all the others, and why, in God's name, do you wanna do your hair like her? My dear grandmother always said, 'My child, from the day they paraded Bona through Chios on a monkey with her buttocks in the air (pardon me, m'lady) wearing a purple frock—I was then at the age of marriage—nobody ever wore that colour.''

'Well, I suppose, no matter how awkward the fashion might seem, if one wants to be considered sophisticated, one needs to follow it; listen to this embarrassing story! ...Easy, Ploumou, don't tear my hair so much! My head is not the back of your father's donkey.'

'Oh, m'lady, don't be so touchy; pain is the price of beauty...tell me what you wanted to say.'

'Well, Ploumou, a certain lady in Paris who was very fashionable did her hair every day the way it was advertised in the magazines. But her husband, not wanting to bear the costs any longer, tried to make her change her mind, as many other foolish men had tried before. Therefore, he asked the editor of the most fashionable magazine to write that the latest trend was to wear a big radish in the hair instead of flowers.

'The lady read this, and as she was going to attend a very splendid ball that evening, she purchased the biggest radish she could find and put it on her head. Everybody laughed at her, but the poor woman believed she had done everything right because she had read about the latest fashion and followed it.

'Her husband, on the contrary, was as guilty as the public prosecutor, who did not take care to censor the newspaper before it was even printed and to prosecute with the utmost vigour the editor who had dared to insult, so flagrantly, the beauty-loving, elegant lady.'

'Ah, ah, ah, stupidity grows like mushrooms these days. The poor thing escaped with a black eye.'

'Why do you say that Ploumou?'

'Because the article merely mentioned a radish. Had it claimed that it was in fashion to carry a bouzouki from Chios on her head, she would have broken her neck under the weight.'

'Give me the looking glass so I can see what you did... Oh, almost the same.'

'Yes, the same; nothing is missing!'

'Move the parting of the hair a bit in this direction, will you? It covers my face too much.'

'Immediately, m'lady, here!'

'Well done! Now put here, near the parting, this rose, fetch my *Eau de Cologne* so I can wash myself, and quickly prepare yesterday's dress for me to put on... Did my aunty send Yerasimos to tell Kallistratos I expected him about an urgent matter?'

'Don't worry, m'lady; your aunty took care of the matter first thing this morning, before even saying her prayers—it was as if she had seen him in her dream. But tell me, was it necessary to fetch Kallistratos so early in the morning when the most dashing young men of Athens are your lovers? You always mock him and put him on a spit with your aunty. You laugh about him; you call him names, say that he is a boor, a buffoon and stupid and looks like his monkey, but when he comes, you alter your attitude immediately. You make curtsies and say that you are in love with him. You say that when you don't see him, you don't eat, and do many other things.'

'Ah, my poor, dear Ploumou, you don't know this world. Of course, I know better than to fall in love with this imbecile whose very sight brings me revulsion. Mind you, Kallistratos is wealthy and stupid, a godsend to any woman in a fashionable society. Does that answer your question?'

'More or less, but...'

At this moment, the noise of the carriage, which had stopped in front of Soultana's house, could be heard in the room and put an end to the conversation.

'Hurry to him, Ploumou, and ask him to wait a little while in the hall. I am coming.'

'Speaking of the devil!' sighed the lithe maid while rushing out of the boudoir and closing the door behind her.

12. The True Love of Fashionable Women, or the Yellow Ball Gown

Kallistratos waited impatiently in the hall where he sat down with Soultana's mother, always fiddling with his broad, pleated necktie and straw-coloured gloves. Occasionally, he played with the locks on his head or the monocle, fastened with a golden chain around his neck. He was beating the ground with his elegant walking stick, moving his head theatrically while answering the old woman's questions. He often gave answers beside the point, as he had his eyes and mind fixed on the door through which the idol of his heart would emerge. Finally, light footsteps and the graceful swish of silken fabric sweeping the floor announced the presence of the lovely maiden.

Kallistratos, as he stood up and bent forward to greet the approaching Soultana deferentially, accidentally pushed his hat that lay on the table. This, in turn, pushed a crystal vase filled with flowers, which broke, causing the flowers and the water to spread all over the table and the floor rug. Therefore, Kallistratos interrupted his courteous greeting and rushed across the hall after his floating hat. The darling Soultana hid her displeasure at the loss of the beautiful vase, a treasured gift from the secretary of the French Embassy—but the look she gave her mummy revealed what a boorish oaf she considered him.

She extended her hand towards him with a forced and graceful smile and feigned indifference, saying, 'Oh, this is a trifling matter, M'sieur Kallistratos. For some time now, I was meaning to remove this vase and replace it with a Chinese one, like the ones they bring from England, truly *le dernier cri*.'

Kallistratos mumbled something that made no sense, to make excuses for himself. He only recovered from his shock thanks to the repeated assurances of the dear Soultana about the triviality of the matter. He sat

https://doi.org/10.11647/OBP.0493.12

next to her on the sofa and started to adjust everything in his attire that was dishevelled from the incident, and after a few minutes, Kallistratos broke the silence.

He started to pay her compliments, but the lovely Soultana smiled, turning gracefully and saying, 'It seems to me, m'sieur, that you are in a zesty mood today.'

'And why would that be, mademoiselle?' he asked, touching his beard and twirling his moustache.

'How else can you praise my attire today when I am neither properly dressed nor combed?'

'That is strange, as your hair appears so wonderfully made, the tresses so perfect, one could swear that you just had been prepared by the personal coiffeuse of the Grande Duchesse d' Orléans.'

'How much you show that you're a gentleman of the polite society who has always lived in the capital of elegance and style. However, this time, you are deceived. The deception is because my hair is naturally smooth and soft, and also because I did not lay my head to rest yesterday but stayed awake all night so that my coiffe remained unaltered.'

'I guess you were reading the comments on the national budget by the famous economist from the Peloponnese.'

'Oh, oh, more substantial cares than the expertise of an economist have tormented my anguished soul,' sighed Soutlana while cunningly making a sign to her mummy, who in turn pretended to have heard the maid calling and said, 'I am coming! I am coming, Ploumou!' and left the room.

'It upsets me, dear Soultana,' said Kallistratos, 'that I might be, and against my will, the primary cause of your sighs and sleepless nights. Of course, I do desire to be loved by you, but not that this be the cause of your ill health, God forbid. Health is the most important gift.'

Now, Soultana, though so much versed in the art of beguiling and deceiving, almost burst into laughter when she heard the cause that Kallistratos blamed for her sleeplessness. But seizing this new opportunity with her quick wits, she answered, 'Alas, when a sensitive female devotes herself to the man whom her heart has chosen once and for all, she considers as a blessing everything that she has to go through: sorrow and misfortunes, hunger, thirst, storms. Neither fire nor the sword can make her waver in her unchangeable resolution.

When smitten with pure love, even death is for her a blessing, because the image of her idol always accompanies her.

'Oh, my dear Kallistratos, to experience love, one must be a woman. We alone were born for this; some even seem, in this day and age of corruption and selfishness, to be destined, as indeed I am, to prove that we were created to be the very model of honest devotion and the most tender feelings of selfless love. This was the girl I was when I first set eyes on you. My heart compelled me to love you; I was subjected to all trials and torments.

'Yes, my heart, through which I first felt the fiery arrows of Amor piercing for your sake. But what hurts me are the wicked tongues of men who pour poison into my cup of happiness, whose bitterness I could swallow without complaining if they had not soiled most wickedly the only thing in life I treasure: your name!

'After the royal ball that took place three days ago, they seized the opportunity to hurl the bitterest insults against you since they saw me dressed. They claimed that 'neither his noble pedigree, nor his European upbringing and manners, nor his excellent qualifications, his connection and substantial education should allow Kallistratos to let the woman he claims he loves present herself at a royal ball so inelegant and dressed, while he is the most admired person at the royal court.'

'This malicious tongue-wagging tore up my heart, I assure you, my dear Kallistratos. And since it is my greatest pleasure to sacrifice everything in your name, I decided to end the gossip of our envious enemies and mortgage my house, the house my late father left me as my only dowry. Thus, I obtained a loan of 10,000 drachmas to order a yellow dress from Paris, similar to the one the Queen wore at the ball, and the other necessities for a splendid appearance worthy of the name of the man my heart adores.'

Having spoken thus, the dear Soultana cast a passionate gaze, accompanied by sighs, towards Kallistratos and used her white handkerchief, pretending to wipe her tears. The charming words of the Soultana; the ardent love Kallistratos believed this lovely young woman held for him, making her burn with desire; the injustice of the whole affair; the sigh and the tears of his beloved, which Kallistratos too had imagined flowing. All this excited the imagination and the vanity of this son of a farmer from Phrygia, who felt insulted by the abuses heaped on his beloved because she did not have a luxurious gown.

'How preposterous!' he cried out. 'It is merely a luxurious dress, and you waste away and are saddened about something that can be obtained with money, a matter on which I am prepared to sacrifice the world.

'And how can it be that you confess your ardent love for me on the one hand and then tell me that you intend to mortgage your house when my entire fortune is at your disposal? When I am ready to be sold as a slave, if necessary, so that you might not be wanting in anything?

'Your behaviour shows that you don't know yet that my love is not inferior to your love for me, and never will I accept the mortgaging of your property; this would be the greatest insult to me.

'Tomorrow, a ship embarks for Marseille. Now, quickly write down an order, not only for the yellow dress, the same one the Queen wore, but also for the matching jewellery and anything else you require so that I can send it to Paris immediately. I can assure you that at the next royal ball, you will outshine the Queen of Greece and all the queens of the world, including even Queen Pomare of Tahiti.'

'I will gladly accept your offer to send to Paris if this will make you happy. But only under the condition that you will receive my property as surety.'

'I implore you, my darling little Soultana, do not insult my love with offers not befitting my status. On the contrary, I beg of you to accept this finery as a small token from me for your upcoming birthday.'

'Never, never in my life could I accept this!'

But Kallistratos fell to his knees in front of her and, having placed her hand tightly in his, cried out, 'I will not rise, cruel mistress, until you accept my offer.'

Now Soultana was initially set upon prolonging her charade, but having felt her hand being pressed too hard between those of her sturdy Phrygian lover, cried out, 'Oh... I agree to whatever you want,' while Kallistratos kissed the almost crushed hand of his lover, then stood up. But his sudden leap caused his *sous-pieds* to break, and when Kallistratos realised this, he protested, 'See, cruel lady, how much of a cripple my love for you has made me.'

The lovely Soultana smiled gracefully while her mummy—who seemed to have followed the whole scene from outside and now perceived that the charade was coming to an end—entered the room and escorted Kallistratos to the other room to mend the broken *sous-pieds*. In the meantime, little Soultana went into her boudoir to write her Paris order.

After a short while, Kallistratos returned to the hall where the mirthful, joyous Soultana received him. He took the note and left, yet while he was still walking down the stairs, Soultana let herself fall onto a sofa and, crying with laughter, exclaimed again and again, 'The fool is in the sack; the fool is in the sack! At the next ball of the Court, I will wear the same yellow dress the Queen wore three days ago.'

13. The Journey of Xouth with Maloukatos and Ligarides

Kallistratos came back from the beautiful Soultana's house at about three in the afternoon and, as far as one could tell from his earnest mien, either the conversation with that young lady had been extremely serious, or something else unpleasant had happened or yet some other curious matter was consuming all of Kallistratos' thoughts.

As soon as he entered, he ordered dinner and ate alone, in great haste and much earlier than usual. Then he summoned his private secretary, the Marquis de la Tourné-Broch, and requested that the daily reading of documents be adjourned. However, he did dictate a letter to his banker in Paris, asking the messenger for the payment of 25,000 francs. Kallistratos signed the letter and sent it to the First Secretary of the Embassy of France with another letter, in which he enclosed the note of order from Soultana.

When this business was taken care of, Kallistratos called Xouth and bade him continue with his story. So, the latter continued with his story:

It was, therefore, decided that I should join the party of my masters in the journey to be undertaken, and I beamed with joy. On the one hand, I had escaped the danger of being deported to the zoo of the pasha of Smyrna, and on the other, I believed I would profit from the travel, as indeed I would.

As Old Maloukas truly possessed the 'two necessary virtues of any traveller: prudence and charity,' as the wise Koraes once said, I learned more things by observing him in the shape of a monkey than by travelling as a European visitor.

©2025 Pitsipios (text)
Christodoulides (trans. & notes), CC BY 4.0   https://doi.org/10.11647/OBP.0493.13

So, having embarked on a steamer from Smyrna, we sailed for Alexandria where the consul general of Greece to Alexandria hosted Mr Maloukatos and Master Ligarides, who was—we reveal this on the side—one of the most favoured courtiers in the Court of the Satrap of Egypt.

During the first days of our stay in Alexandria, the consul, having seen me, said to Ligarides that he wished to show me to the wife of his nephew, who was English and would indeed find delight with me. Moreover, Master Ligarides, being who he is, took me with him one evening to a diplomatic dinner where the consul had also invited my master.

As we entered the reception hall with Mr Maloukatos and Master Ligarides, everybody greeted me courteously, while the said Englishwoman was especially friendly and placed me next to her. But after a little while, I saw a small, unsightly little hag entering, awkwardly overdressed and tawdry, whom everybody present greeted most deferentially.

The wife of the nephew of the Consul General of Greece, whose naive and polite demeanour bore witness both to the upbringing of an Englishwoman and to an intimate knowledge of true polite behaviour, stood up gracefully and greeted the old hag, being hostess to the party, and extended her hand and asked her to sit next to her.

After the usual trivial compliments, I gathered that this shapeless mass of bones was the wife of the consul of Naples in Alexandria. The polite hostess introduced my masters to her, and afterwards she introduced me as a curiosity, a monkey raised in England!

But whereas the consul's wife paid no further attention to my masters, she immediately came to sit next to me and exclaimed all the time, 'What a beautiful animal!' while tenderly caressing my chin and my feet, which she kissed, perhaps to fawn upon the proud English hostess.

Though these disgusting displays of deference of the old sycophant greatly displeased me at first, my discomfort immediately turned into surprise when I recognised a ring with a precious ancient stone on her finger. The same ring I had bought once in Smyrna, which I kept in one of the two trinket boxes, surreptitiously taken from me from that hotel in Paris, owned by the fat man who had once served in the Garde Nationale during the glorious days of Napoleon.

Thunderstruck, I turned my gaze towards the face of the ugly hag, and my initial joy turned into horror when I carefully studied her face and discovered under the prune-like and shrunken features, brought about by the decaying power of time, the countenance of my wicked, impostor sister. The 'Countess Avendrote'! The female crook who had robbed me in Paris and who was the primary cause of my undoing!

I let slip an unconscious howl like a lunatic and stood up like a real orangutan, grinding my teeth. I was ready to assail the hateful creature and tear her into pieces, had the screams of her and the other guests not led Master Ligarides to grab me by the neck and drag me out of the reception hall to hand me over to his servant. He, in turn, assisted by the servants of the consul, placed me on a bier and carried me to the hotel, almost unconscious and out of breath from the violent shock that the sight of the perpetrator of all my misfortunes had caused.

When I regained my consciousness and the whole extent of the horror of the earlier scene passed again before my eyes, it was almost midnight. But when I came to my senses again, I also remembered my previous perils—that, because of my naivety and the honest fondness and devotion I showed towards the phoney sister of mine, I had fallen into the cunning web of this female crook and ended up, on account of my misery, as a common murderer, sentenced to atone to God. I lived for so many years as a wild beast in the desert, passed from master to master in the shape of an ape. In contrast, this despicable hag succeeded in becoming the wife of the Consul General of Naples, living in high society, enjoying the attention and the dinners. Heavens above: is this justice?

During the whole night, I was tormented by gloomy thoughts while the sudden remembrance of my calamities reopened old wounds. My mental and bodily powers were so exhausted that the next morning, I was lying like a dead man, unable to move and burning with a strong fever. Master Ligarides, who had noticed this serious and sudden affliction, hurried to call a much-respected doctor of Alexandria, an Italian, called Fysicha, who came to the house and, when he saw Mr Maloukatos, sitting in his chair and smoking his pipe, ran towards him, took the old man's hand and counted his pulse.

Your servant was right to tell me that you are suffering from a strong fever, since your pulse betrays a great heat indeed. In addition, it appears you suffer either from stomachitis, a cold, haemorrhoids, a nervous affliction, a headache, gastritis or diarrhoea. Therefore, I believe that you must immediately shed some blood, and if it does not work, I will give you a strong cleanser. If this does not work either, I prescribe Chenin. If not even that can cure the affliction, then tomorrow I will prepare a sweet potion made of all the known and unknown herbs, of which you will have to take one dose every quarter of an hour. And if we cannot lower the strong fever with that either, you must take a cold bath immediately and use compresses of snap on the neck and cockroaches around your heels, and if that does not help either...'

'Most excellent of doctors,' Old Maloukatos interrupted the unabating blabbing of that Hippocrates of Alexandria, 'it is not me who is the patient, it is an ape from the family of the orangutans, which my nephew owns...'

'Oh!' the doctor shouted out, gesticulating wildly, interrupting Old Maloukatos in turn, and beating the ground with his luxurious and heavy stick. 'This is quite a different matter. I am not a doctor for apes. I know how to cure camels, donkeys and the poodles of the ladies and the nobility of Alexandria. The horses, the apes and the ladies are under the medical jurisdiction of my esteemed colleague Xylokaias.

'Between us, we have divided up, for some time now, all the patients of Egypt according to their species. And since one respects the sphere of the other, and because your patient does not have the honour to be counted among my patients, *et cetera*, my respected science is in this case not applicable, for as the Roman doctor says, '*Scorbuto laborantibus hoc est dyspepsia aut urgent diarrhoea cum doloribus abdominis, aut altero quoddam morbo affectis, etc.*' Do you understand Latin? My deepest respects, my lords; I make haste to call my friend Xylokaikas, who will cure *de lege artis*, the ape of your nephew. For this visit's payment, I beg you to send it to my house.'

Having spoken thus, he rushed out, gesticulating wildly, mumbling some medical Latin and pretending not to hear Old Maloukatos, who was shouting behind him, asking him not to trouble the excellent Xylokaikas since the ape of his nephew does not need a doctor anymore.

Meanwhile, Master Ligarides, having heard from the hotelier of another famous doctor in Alexandria, called Kalathounas, hurried to ask him for help. This doctor came whistling and greeted them with a nodding of his head. As soon as he came in, he placed a large box of some kind that he was carrying under his arm. Then, he sat down in the armchair, crossed his legs, took a white handkerchief from his pocket, and blew his nose, loud as a trumpet. He took the large snuffbox into his hands and, taking the lid with dexterity, opened it and filled his two big nostrils, then used his handkerchief to remove the tobacco that had fallen out, then asked both Mr Maloukatos and Master Ligarides, 'Who of you is the patient?'

'Neither, most excellent doctor,' Master Ligarides replied. 'It is my ape who has suffered greatly since yesterday.'

'It makes no difference to me,' the doctor replied. 'For, since illnesses afflict man and beast likewise, and every creature finds cure in his likeness, our homoeopathic science does not distinguish between animals and men as regards the method of therapy, neither in the substance nor the formula.'

'Do you not wish, most excellent doctor, to come into the patient's chamber to look at him?'

'Tell me only what kind of affliction it is.'

'High fever,' Master Ligarides repeated.

'This suffices,' the homoeopathic doctor stated. 'So, the fever will be cured with one milligram of a drop of the liquid stored in the thirteenth row of my box under the number 322. You must dilute it in four pounds of clear water and give it to the patient for four days. After this period, the medicine will start to work, and the patient's condition will visibly improve.'

Having spoken thus, he took a key from his pocket and opened the box on the table. He found the little phial with the number 322 written on it, which he opened very carefully, and took one drop with his syringe, which he then placed into a cup, and handed it to Master Ligarides with these words: 'Take great care that the division of the water into four equal parts is done with precision; otherwise, there will be no hope for the patient. As for the cost of my visit, it is four distels, for I am never greedy.' Having finished his sentence, he stretched his hand towards Mr Maloukatos.

'But, Sir, I heard that a fever can easily become an inflammation. In how many days can this happen?'

'In three or four days at most,' the doctor answered.

'But, most excellent doctor,' Mr Maloukatos asked, 'if this miraculous medicine of yours will start to work only after forty days, is the patient not at risk of dying if an inflammation appears?'

'Of course, but the superb Samuel Hahnemann states in his treatise that there is no other way of treating the fever. Moreover, my long experience only confirms this opinion.

'Be aware that we, who follow the great theory of this great teacher, are not like the charlatans who follow Hippocrates; liars and ignorant, taxing society most shamelessly and causing destruction and loss everywhere instead of gain.'

In the meantime, Doctor Xylokaikas came into the room, having been sent by his friend Fysichas, and after hearing Kalathountas' last remarks, he got terribly angry. He grabbed him by the neck with his sturdy hand and shook him.

'How dare you?' he said. 'How ignorant to insult the wise disciples of Hippocrates—you, whose entire learning fits into a box? Moreover, most of all, you slander us in the very house where you have no right to be in the first place. For the doctor who was called here first, Fysichas, having discovered that this was about an ill ape and not wanting to interfere with my sacred jurisdiction, sent for the only specialist in the whole of Egypt and its vicinities for the afflictions of the apes.'

'It matters little to me, stupid Xylokaikas,' Kalathountas retorted. 'If you are a doctor of the apes or the monkeys, I will show you that I can make you stay in bed for one entire month. Like the time when they crushed your head since you dared boo out the beautiful Polana while everybody applauded her.'

At this, he hurled his snuffbox into his face, causing him a heavy blow, and he immediately turned towards the stairs. But Xylokaikas, who had his entire face covered in tobacco, grabbed Kalathountas' box with the medicines and, rushing to follow him on the stairs, threw it at the head of the fleeing pupil of Dr Hahnemann.

The two continued their assaults on the street while abusing each other with the kind of lofty expressions that only those with similarly high education can use.

Meanwhile, Old Maloukatos closed the door and turned to Master Ligarides. 'These people are unworthy of curing either man or beast but only able to live with wild donkeys and pigs in the mountains.'

Towards evening, the Greek consul called upon my masters and, as soon as he heard from Maloukatos what had happened, he recommended to

Ligarides the chief doctor of his excellency, the Carabiniero, a Frenchman, whom he called immediately through his interpreter.

This man was most polite and grand, and, after the usual exchange of pleasantries, he asked Old Maloukatos if, during his travels, he had by any chance heard people talking about the marvellous book he had published about the plague and his theory about that illness.

When Old Maloukatos replied he had not, Carabiniero frowned. 'I want,' he said, 'to give you a small sample of my most worthy and wise system, in which I fairly and squarely prove that the plague neither existed nor was contagious in any way.'

And he began to expatiate for so long that Old Maloukatos and his nephew almost fell asleep, when an employee of the Greek consulate hastily entered and said that His Highness called for the head doctor Carabiniero immediately. The latter paused his wise speech, asked Maloukatos to be excused, and left straight away, promising to return the next day to see the patient.

However, the next day, the consul informed my masters that the head doctor Carabiniero, having left his hotel, carelessly touched a man afflicted with the plague and caught it himself. I was not lying in bed in a dire condition. So, having managed to escape the hands of the doctors on account of their fights and sluggishness, I got rid of my fever on my own and regained my health without their help.

14. The Four Great Trials of My 'Sister' in Three Hours

After my recovery, I heard from the conversations of Old Maloukatos and Master Ligarides with various dignitaries that the female impostor who had robbed me in Paris became the object of gossip in Alexandria from the very first day she set foot in that city. On one occasion, she would say that she descended from the family of the Shah of Persia, and then she would claim to be from a ruling family of India. On another occasion, she stated that she was the daughter of an English lord. Then again, she claimed to be the widow of an Italian prince.

All these confusing and contradictory accounts made the people of Alexandria suspicious, and everybody longed to know the nationality, pedigree and religion of this curious hag, about whom nothing was known except that she was not even the legal wife of the consul of Naples. At length, everybody suspected from her words and actions that she was not a Christian but was born a Jew. Nonetheless, the rest of her life story remained hidden in a shroud of mystery.

Finally, the death of her alleged husband, which occurred while we were staying in Alexandria, brought to light a big part of her true story and dispelled all doubts about her true confession. The consul saw that his end was near and, wanting to leave the woman with whom he had spent so many years a fortune and social standing through her bearing of his name, he called the Catholic church priests and asked them to marry them. However, knowing precisely the mysterious history of that woman, they refused to marry a Christian without having her baptised first.

But since time was pressing and no delay was possible, as the pangs of death had already set in and it was clear to the consul that his life would finish soon, the woman consented to be baptised. Thus, within three hours, that curious female was catechised, baptised, married and became a widow.

©2025 Pitsipios (text)
Christodoulides (trans. & notes), CC BY 4.0

https://doi.org/10.11647/OBP.0493.14

15. Master Ligarides Is Writing His Fashionable Travelogue

On the day before we departed from Alexandria, a warm wind set in during the morning. The wind came from the equator and was stiflingly hot. The natives call it 'chamsin.' It feels like hot lava and covers the air and the sun in the sand it carries from the desert, blackening everything and creating an atmosphere of death. Moreover, this wind becomes lethal to animals and plants if its destructive breath lasts too long.

But through some divine providence, this destructive wind does not usually last more than twenty-four hours. During that time, the inhabitants of Alexandria—especially foreigners—were well-advised to stay inside their houses with all the windows and shutters hermetically locked, preventing the poisonous chamsin from entering as much as possible.

Naturally, my masters—being warned that the wind was imminent by the consul of Greece—shut all doors and windows and stayed inside for the entire day. And Master Ligarides, having nothing else to do, remembered, following the custom of European travellers, to write in his diary about his travel to Alexandria. Therefore, he placed a big city map on the large table and gathered many books by various English and French travellers around it. He started to peruse the books and tried to pin the position of the various monuments of Alexandria on the map. Then he began walking back and forth through the room, perplexed and gesticulating awkwardly. He called me and ordered me to summon the servant, whom he bade call the hotelier Agkopes, an Armenian, as well as an employer of the consulate, Suleiman Aga. These two men Master Ligarides had selected, in tune with the European fashion, as advisors for this important memoir about Alexandria.

When they entered, he spoke thus, 'I wish to write an important memoir about Alexandria and the whole of Egypt, and I believe you two

https://doi.org/10.11647/OBP.0493.15

are the most suitable to help me because of your first-hand knowledge about this matter, which you have acquired during your long stay here.'

'If I understand correctly, sir,' the hotelier replied, 'you wish to write a diary of your visit to Egypt. I can assure you, sir, that I am not only in a position to give you the most precise advice, but I can also lift from you the burden of having to write it up. Since I have already written the travel diary that all the French and English visitors simply copy from me, each one merely changing the main names and certain dates.' On finishing his sentence, he rushed out and came back immediately with his blueprint of a diary of Egypt.

When I perceived Master Ligarides taking the book and perusing it with a ridiculous seriousness, I recalled that I had once worked similarly during my travels to Greece and Turkey, using the sources gathered in Smyrna by Don Giurumis and Avraamatsos, and I too had paid for them.

I sighed now, seeing my master overcome by the same folly, and felt genuinely concerned lest, at the end of the day, he too met a certain *comtesse*—a long-lost sister—and a fat hotelier who allowed him to receive the kind attention of a certain fashionable public prosecutor.

For the present, anyway, Master Ligarides was greatly pleased with the fascinating content of the exemplary diary and, turning towards the hotelier, said, 'This is all fine, but there is one more obstacle, and I wish you could help me with this. You know very well that European travellers habitually sign their names on the monuments they have visited, or are supposed to have visited, in any case. Since I now wish to inscribe my name on the tallest pyramid, on the top of the *stele* of Pompey and the 'Needle of Cleopatra,' I ask you to find a skilled craftsman whom I can commission to produce these inscriptions for me.'

'Do not worry about this; my friend Suleiman Agas knows a Jew who specialises in this. He charges one distel per letter. It is a bargain indeed, considering his expenses, his labour and the fact that he is so much in demand for all Europeans. Please, sir, write the inscriptions down on paper so that he might collect them immediately and execute the commission with the utmost perfection. In fact, in my manuscript you will find, my lord, towards the end, various graffiti of illustrious Europeans, which might serve as examples to choose from.'

Master Ligarides was greatly relieved that this difficulty was overcome. Having carefully examined all the graffiti in the book, he decided to copy three yet alter them a little. He asked the hotelier to summon the Jewish contractor to discuss their inscription on each of Egypt's three archaeological monuments.

On top of the Great Pyramid near Cairo, the selected and modified graffito read thus:

> *Ligarides, the son of Venias, preeminent among the travellers of this world, climbed here on 25 April 1835.*

On the top of the stele of Pompey in Alexandria:

> *Ligarides, the son of Venias, climbed here on horseback on 25 April 1835.*

Moreover, in the 'Needle of Cleopatra,' we read:

> *Ligarides of Vanias visited this monument on 25 April 1835 and discovered, assisted by the wise scholia to the Political and Commercial Codex of Dourantos and Pardessios, the needle that Cleopatra used to sew the shirts of Caesar.*

To his surprise, the hotelier Agkopes took the text and counted 342 letters. He then started negotiations in Arabic with Suleiman Aga and the Jewish contractor. After feigned rows and gesticulations between those three honourable men, he turned to Master Ligarides. 'In the end, we agreed that Suleiman Agas would inscribe the three graffiti pieces for only 500 distels, including all costs of material, expenses, labour and the traditional gift to the contractor. This is an excellent price and, please remember, never has a traveller paid less.'

Master Ligarides himself, though he found this price very modest considering the eternal glory that would come from the three inscriptions, realised that his uncle would never pay this amount for the sake of his fame, but did not have this amount himself. Therefore, he was greatly puzzled about how to solve this matter.

But here, the genius of the Armenian hotelier, the Jewish contractor and the employee of the Greek consulate, after renewed deliberation, resolved the matter thus. It was decided that Master Ligarides would sign a debit note to the hotelier for 500 distels, to be paid after the death of Old Maloukatos, with an interest of only twenty percent until the day of payment. At the same time, he would stand as surety in person to the Jewish contractor.

Master Ligarides immediately remembered that once his friend and compatriot, the lawyer Pegadostomides, had advised him similarly and he had accepted the offer gladly. He set up the note of debt, duly signed it, and handed it to the Armenian hotelier. Therefore, the three undertakers of Master Ligarides' journey left at once to fulfil their commission.

16. Maloukatos' Thoughts on the Travelogue of Master Ligarides

When Master Ligarides was left alone, he started to peruse the copy of the *Egyptian Journey* he had received from Ancopes. He copied various bits and pieces from this as well as English and French books. He also wrote down various episodes which he invented himself to imitate the English and French books he had handy. The events he narrated were fictional: some extraordinary, others entirely plausible.

He had already piled up a nauseating and awkward array of mendacious, outlandish and silly tales when Maloukatos entered the room and asked him what had consumed his time, preventing him from appearing all day.

'I was occupied writing up my diary about my journey to Egypt, which I have just finished,' Master Ligarides replied, beaming with pride while pointing to his oeuvre.

Maloukatos took the text into his hands and started reading it. There were moments when the wise old man shook his head in dismay and gesticulated in despair while his face betrayed a sadness on account of his nephew's folly. Having finished reading, he sat on the sofa nearby and asked his nephew to sit beside him.

He spoke thus, 'The education of the wealthy Greeks in my time, Ligarides, consisted solely of reading and writing our language and of practical mathematics. A few were also taught 'dry grammar.' It appears that traditional education, though limited in scope, has been supported and monitored by parents and relatives, which bore fruit. This kind of education fostered reason and turned the young into prudent and useful persons, both for themselves and society. However, ever since it became customary to educate the youth abroad for several years, I noticed that most of those who learn abroad come back ignorant, stupid and

©2025 Pitsipios (text)
Christodoulides (trans. & notes), CC BY 4.0   https://doi.org/10.11647/OBP.0493.16

conceited. Many are corrupted to the core. And to speak the truth, it is not surprising. For these youths arrive in a foreign country whose language they don't know, whose morals and customs are very different from those of their homeland, lacking any guidance, advice and protection. They have enough money at their display, without the fear of shame instilled upon them from the knowledge that their parents and kin know about their follies, being instead unknown in the European cities in which they live. Therefore, they fall in a short period into utter baseness. Instead of devoting their attention to their lessons, they spend their time in useless wanderings, dances, theatres and illicit relationships.

'Meanwhile, they write one letter to their families each month. They start by listing the fifteen disciplines they claim to be occupied with and conclude with the commonplace complaints that their allowance is insufficient for purchasing so many books and paying private tutors. Truthfully, the money is spent on visits to theatres and cafes, and on the most depraved pursuits. During my short stay, I was unfortunate to witness this wicked behaviour of Greek students in Europe and to hear the same account from other compatriots. I already see that since you came back from your extended educational stay in Europe and America, you not only did not benefit but became even more imbecilic and, I am afraid, have acquired more European vices.

'Tell me, pray, how do you hope to benefit from this heap of shameless lies, the nauseating mumbo jumbo and the outlandish aping you put together as a supposed travel journey? You even dare to claim that you wish to publish this for the benefit of mankind!

'Where have you seen the pyramids of Egypt? How were you the first to climb one in 1835, when tens of thousands of people have climbed it throughout the centuries? Is there something more ridiculous than not knowing that the so-called 'Needle of Cleopatra' is an obelisk made of stone, weighing thousands of pounds, and mistaking it for a needle that women use for sewing? Moreover, who will benefit if they read that you ate delicious bananas on 17 April and one of them was very ripe? On 18 April, you dined with the consul of Greece and then went to the Kafenion and played billiards? What is the benefit of knowing that, when you left the Kafenion, you encountered two women from Abyssinia and concluded from their age that they must have been mother and daughter? And many other such trifles. And most of all, they are all preposterous lies!'

'But dear uncle, our compatriot and my friend, Pegadostomides the lawyer, always told me that the social lives of great men must be founded on mendacity. To be happy and admired in the world, one needs to be neither honest nor just nor educated. One must only know how to simulate effectively and incessantly tout one's virtues and abilities. Only then can one gain the most. If, on the other hand, he decides to adhere to the precepts of virtue truly, the remonstrances of his conscience and all its silly precepts will prevent him from all the lucrative enterprises. He himself based all his actions on pretence, lies and deceit and often did marvellously for himself.

'I have known for some time now,' Maloukatos retorted earnestly, 'that these are the principles of this wretched little lawyer. I know that Pegadostomides seems to have, by nature, an evil mind and a twisted disposition. He obviously picked up all the malicious streaks found in Europe without picking up anything beneficial from his American journey.

'In fact, the main reason I recently asked you to come to me was to end your communication with this corrupt man, and I already fear that my foresight will come too late! You know that this calamity is lethal for me since I relied on you for the continuation of my family ever since I was deprived of all hope to find my only daughter and cousin of yours, Marietta.'

Thus, he spoke, and tears rolled down the wrinkled cheeks of the childless man. His reprimands and censure of the morals of Pegadostomides, as well as the name of Marietta, upset Ligarides in the same way that the apparition of the bloodstained victim haunts the murderer. Pale and speechless, he fixed his gaze on the ground. Penitence and corruption contested each other at the bottom of his shallow heart, and sundry opposing reasons alternately took hold of his impressionable soul. Having carefully observed how the voice of conscience had upset Ligarides, it seemed to me that he was ready to throw himself at the feet of his benefactor and to confess everything he knew and did on account of Marietta, and that he would beg for forgiveness for his depravity. However, the hapless old man was right! Circumstances showed that the measure of conscience came too late.

17. The Malady

The next day, we embarked on an English steamer and left Alexandria, and after a few days' journey on a calm sea, we arrived in London. But two days after we arrived in this big city, I fell ill again, with a fever much stronger and more malignant than the one I had suffered in Alexandria. I was in such a wretched condition that I would hardly appear alive, were it not for the fiery heat that my entire body exuded and the heavy panting of my breath.

My lords had called, one by one, many of the Hippocrateses of England. However, all of them came to the safe conclusion, through various lofty and learned syllogisms, first that I suffered from either fever or spleen- or gastro-enteritis or a stroke. Second, that my illness was caused either by a cold, high blood pressure or from the stomach, the change of the climate or, finally, even an unknown cause. Therefore, since my body's natural function was derailed by the effects of said causes, it was necessary to restore this function to its original condition with the aid of science.

But the real misfortune that stemmed from these philosophical thoughts and witty considerations was that the excellent doctors fiercely disagreed about the kind of scientific remedies they might use in the present situation.

Some gave the opinion that, since my illness came from high blood pressure, I would die immediately if I were not taken to the countryside and covered entirely in ice; whereas others claimed that my illness came from a cold and it was therefore imperative that I be put into a warm bath that would make me sweat—for, without this drastic measure, I would also most certainly die.

Another luminary of the medical profession urged that I be made to shed blood immediately. Otherwise, I would die within two hours. Yet another doctor, red-headed with a protruding belly, warned that

https://doi.org/10.11647/OBP.0493.17

even the slightest bloodshed would cause my death, and to prove the infallibility of his expert diagnosis, he beat his hand on the table. He offered to enter a bet of ten pounds of roast beef, asking my masters to embark upon this course of therapy out of curiosity, at least so that his superior expertise might be proven correct.

The dissenting opinions agitated by these choleric British doctors led to fights, with swearing and threats, and the chamber was now more like a pub filled with drunken sailors than a patient's room filled with disciples of the divine science.

At length, thankfully, one doctor—whose voice was the loudest—succeeded in calming down this terrible storm with the following wise words. 'Gentlemen, all of us who are here at present are most excellent, and each one may freely disagree with the others regarding the method of applying the therapy, as this stems from the differences in practice to which each one of us has adhered since leaving university. But since all these methods are recognised as most acceptable by the learned scientists of Europe, they are therefore capable of either bestowing life on the patient or bringing him death, in which case the patient is informed that he has died following *de lege artis*.

'In addition, because each of us adheres to a different therapeutic method, the dignity of our venerated science, the benefit of our practice and our respect towards the patients themselves do not allow anyone to grant primacy to the other's healing method.

'Moreover, since being made doctors, we swore the oath of Hippocrates and pledged that charity will be our sole guide—that we may never be led by our passions, superstitions and private interests—so it is imperative that we are united in focusing on the malady itself, and this can only be achieved through animal magnetism. Therefore, I suggest that we magnetise the patient and induce him to reveal his affliction and the suitable remedy for it.'

A whisper of approval followed the speech of this mesmerist, and the preparations for the magnetism were already underway when Old Maloukatos, who had left the room earlier when the situation was becoming unpleasant, returned and, having learned what the excellent doctors had decided, shook his head with dismay and gave a wry smile. 'Your thoughts about the patient's magnetism are all very well, gentlemen. But pray, in what language do you believe my nephew's ape, once he is put to sleep, will describe to you both his affliction and the most suitable remedy for it?'

Further elaboration on the difficult question put forth by Mr Maloukatos was interrupted, most fortunately for the doctors, by the sudden entrance of Master Ligarides, who handed a letter to his uncle, which the latter read immediately. Having read it, he announced to Master Ligarides that important family interests made it imperative that they both travel to Constantinople. And as it was impossible to carry me with them, as I was lying almost on my deathbed, it was decided that I be transported to the best hospital in London, to which I was brought on that same day, carried on a bier.

As I was lying on the hospital bed, I was surrounded by a crowd of doctors and philosophers of different dispositions, wildly speculating and impatiently waiting, like the nephews and nieces of unmarried uncles, for my imminent death—to benefit science, as they believed, with the findings of my postmortem. And God knows by what monstrosities these *eminences grises* would have further entangled their philosophical theories if they had examined my corpse and discovered that it harboured an organism similar to that of a human being. What philosophical debates! What assails! How many duels and hangings! However, the Lord denied them all this through my recovery.

From the hospital, I was taken by the English master who would later hang himself, and from whom you bought me in London. But what kind of agreement was made with Master Ligarides, and how I passed into his ownership, I could never find out. My English master was so disposed towards lying that he sometimes talked about me and said he had caught me while I was sleeping under a tree in Africa, where he used to hunt.

At other times, he would claim that I was following him in the deserts of Arabia and he captured me out of self respect for his free British spirit, and other such preposterous lies, so that I myself almost ended up forgetting the real story of my life.

Such was the sequence of events from that fateful day on 15 March 1825, from God's will for me to atone for the foul murder of my benefactor until I passed into your ownership, and until the moment when God's grace granted me forgiveness for my horrible crime and gave me back the gift of speech. Having gone into my room on that day,

I locked myself inside and I praised the infinite compassion of the Lord, who did not wish death on the sinner. I hope that, in the future, made wise by my calamities, I will appear useful to society by virtuous living and through the little advice I can give to the younger generation on account of my many trials. If I may, I have much to say to you about your comportment and how it needs to be reformed.

But we can defer to a more suitable moment, in this matter. I already know that you will not deny me the following favour: you know that here I am, known by everybody as an ape, and this strange transformation into a human will cause a huge interest and will bring unbearable harassment to me. Therefore, I beg you to grant me permission and the means to embark on a journey to Syros, perhaps the most civilised city in Greece. After I have dressed up and made myself up like a human, I wish to come to Athens and end my days near you, striving to make myself useful to Your Lordship. I wish for these things, and I beseech you not to divulge the secret of my transformation until my return.

'As far as the last matter is concerned,' Kallistratos replied, 'rest assured since I am among the ablest diplomats of the Megali Idea,[1] and I know how to keep a secret even if its airing is called for. I grant your request and give you 500 distels for your immediate expenses. You are free to go to Syros or wherever you wish.'

The next day, Xouth embarked on an Austrian steamer and left for Syros.

(To be continued.)

---

1   Megali Idea, lit. 'Great Idea,' referred to the political ideology dominant
     throughout the nineteenth and early twentieth centuries which claimed that,
     eventually, all formerly Greek-speaking territories of the Ottoman Empire should
     be brought under Greek control, thus reviving the Byzantine Empire.

Selected Bibliography

Primary Sources

Works by Iakovos Pitsipios

Pitzipios, J. G. (1855). *L'Eglise Oriental, première partie*. Imprimerie de la propagande.

Pitsipios, I. (1848). 'Xouth, the Ape'. *Αποθήκη των Τερπνών και Ωφελίμων Γνώσεων* [The Storehouse of Delightful and Useful Knowledge].

Pitsipios, I. (1995) [1848]. *Η ορφανή της Χίου ή ο θρίαμβος της αρετής – Ο Πίθηκος Ξούθ ή τα ήθη του αιώνος* [The Orphan of Chios or the Triumph of Virtue – Xouth, the Ape, or the Morals of the Century] (D. Tziovas, ed.). Ουρανή.

Pitsipios, I. (1995) [1848]. *Ο πίθηκος Ξουθ ή τα ήθη του αιώνος* [Xouth, the Ape, or the Morals of the Century] (N. Vagenas, ed.). Νεφέλη.

Pitsipios, I. (2020) [1848]. *πίθηκος Ξουθ ή Τα ήθη του αιώνος* [Xouth, the Ape, or the Morals of the Century]. Ανοικτή Βιβλιοθήκη [Open Library]. https://www.openbook.gr/o-pithikos-xoyth/; https://doi.org/10.11647/OBP.0493#resources

Other Primary Sources

Defoe, D. (2009) [1722]. *Moll Flanders*. Oxford World's Classics.

Dickens, C. (with Slater, M.). (1991) [1849–50]. *David Copperfield*. Everyman's Library Classics Series.

Fielding, H. (with Rawson, C.). (1991) [1749]. *Tom Jones*. Everyman's Library Classics Series.

Goethe, J. W. v. (2009) [1795–96]. *Wilhelm Meisters Lehrjahre*. Suhrcamp.

Schiller, F. (1993) [1795]. 'Über naive und sentimentalische Dichtung, *Sämtliche Werke* (G. Fricke & H.t G. Göpfert, eds). Hauser.

Sterne, L. (1768). *A Sentimental Journey through France and Italy*. T. Becket and P.A. De Hondt.

Voltaire, François-Marie Arouet, de (1759). *Candide ou L'Optimisme*. Cramer.

Secondary Sources

Achilles Tatius (with Morales, H.). (2002). *Leucippe and Clitophon*, translated with notes by T. Whitmarsh. Oxford University Press.

Apuleius (2008). *The Golden Ass*, translated by P.G. Walsh. Penguin.

Bakhtin, M.M. (1981). *The Dialogic Imagination*, translated by C. Emerson & M. Holquist (M. Holquist, Ed.) University of Texas Press.

Bakhtin, M.M. (1986). *Speech Genres and Other Essays*, translated by Vern W. McGee (C. Emerson and M. Holquist, eds). University of Texas Press.

Borghart, P. and De Temmerman, K. (2010). 'From Novelistic Romance to Romantic Novel: The Revival of the Ancient Adventure Chronotope in Byzantine and Modern Greek Literature'. *Journal of Mediterranean Studies*, *19*(1), 43–68.

Fairey, J. (2013). 'Failed Nations and Usable Pasts: Byzantium as Transcendence in the Writings of Iakovos Pitsipios Bey'. In O. Delouis, A. Couderc and P. Guran (eds), *Héritages de Byzance en Europe du Sud-Est à l'époque moderne et contemporaine*. Ecole française d'Athènes. (pp. 23–44). https://doi.org/10.4000/books.efa.9340

Iatrou, M. (2017). 'Human Apes and the Dual Self: Notes on the Intertext of Ο Πίθηκος Ξουθ (Xouth the Ape) by Iakovos Pitsipios'. *Neogreca Bohemica, 17*, 9–29.

O'Neill, K.L. (2003). 'The Unfinished Ape: Mediation and Modern Greek Identity in Iakovos Pitsipios's Ο Πίθηκος Ξούθ'. *Journal of Modern Greek Studies, 21*(1), 67–111. https://doi.org/10.1353/mgs.2003.0007

Reardon, B.P. (with Morgan, J.R.). (2019). *Collected Ancient Greek Novels*. University of California Press.

Rebig, G. (1972). *Der Halbbruder des Dichters*. Athenäum.

Roilos, P. (2003). 'The Poetics of Mimicry: Pitzipios' Ο Πίθηκος Ξούθ and the Beginnings of the Modern Greek Novel'. In A. Stathakopoulou and G. Nagy (eds), *Modern Greek Literature: Critical Essays* (pp. 62–78). Routledge.

Σέρβου, Μ. (1997). Οι εξομολογήσεις ενός πιθήκου και ο Ιάκωβος Πιτζιπιός. [The Confessions of an Ape and Iakovos Pitsipios] Ν. Βαγενάς (επιμ), [N. Vagensas, ed.] *ΑΠΟ ΤΟΝ ΛΕΑΝΔΡΟ ΣΤΟΝ ΛΟΥΚΗ ΛΑΡΑ Μελέτες για την πεζογραφία της περιόδου 1830-1880* (pp. 93–102). [From *Leandros* to *Loukis Laras*. Studies on the Prosa of the Period 1830-1880] Πανεπιστημιακές Εκδόσεις Κρήτης [University of Crete Press]

Τζιόβας, Δ. (2003). Ο αποσυνάγωγος Ιάκωβος Γ. Πιτζιπίος: ηθική και μεταμόρφωση. [The Pariah Iakovos Pitsipios: Morals and Transformation.] In Δ. Τζιόβας (επιμ.), [D. Tziovas, ed.] *Κοσμοπολίτες και αποσυνάγωγοι. Μελέτες για την ελληνική πεζογραφία και κριτική (1830–1930)* [Cosmopolitans and Pariahs. Studies in Greek Prose and Criticism (1830–1930)] (pp. 21–109). Μεταίχμιο.

About the Team

Alessandra Tosi was the managing editor for this book.

Annie Hine proof-read this manuscript.

Jeevanjot Kaur Nagpal designed the cover. The cover was produced in InDesign using the Fontin font.

Annie typeset the book in InDesign. The main text font is Tex Gyre Pagella and the heading font is Californian FB.

The conversion to the PDF and HTML editions was performed with open-source software and other tools freely available on our GitHub page at https://github.com/OpenBookPublishers.

Jeremy Bowman created the EPUB.

Hannah Shakespeare was in charge of marketing.

This book was peer-reviewed by two anonymous referees. Experts in their field, these readers donated their time to help ensure the academic rigour of our books. We are grateful for their generous and invaluable contributions.

This book need not end here...

Share

All our books — including the one you have just read — are free to access online so that students, researchers and members of the public who can't afford a printed edition will have access to the same ideas. This title will be accessed online by hundreds of readers each month across the globe: why not share the link so that someone you know is one of them?

This book and additional content is available at
https://doi.org/10.11647/OBP.0493

Donate

Open Book Publishers is an award-winning, scholar-led, not-for-profit press making knowledge freely available one book at a time. We don't charge authors to publish with us: instead, our work is supported by our library members and by donations from people who believe that research shouldn't be locked behind paywalls.

Join the effort to free knowledge by supporting us at
https://www.openbookpublishers.com/support-us

We invite you to connect with us on our socials!

BLUESKY

@openbookpublish
.bsky.social

MASTODON

@OpenBookPublish
@hcommons.social

LINKEDIN

open-book-publishers

Read more at the Open Book Publishers Blog
https://blogs.openbookpublishers.com

You may also be interested in:

That Greece Might Still Be Free
The Philhellenes in the War of Independence
William St Clair; introduction by Roderick Beaton

https://doi.org/10.11647/OBP.0001

Hyperion, or the Hermit in Greece
Translated by Howard Gaskill

https://doi.org/10.11647/OBP.0160

Byron and Trinity
Memorials, Marbles and Ruins
Edited by Adrian Poole

https://doi.org/10.11647/OBP.0399

www.ingramcontent.com/pod-product-compliance
Lightning Source LLC
Chambersburg PA
CBHW061525020726
47502CB00006B/2246